SUMMONING CHAOS

WHAT HAPPENS WHEN A BORED HUMAN SUMMONS A DEMON?
CHAOS!

STELLA RAINBOW

Warning:

This book contains material that is intended for a mature, adult audience. It contains graphic language, explicit sexual content and adult situations.

Trigger Warning:

Brief mention of past sexual assault.

contents

Dedicated to:
Sta'Cee, for supporting me on Patreon. Thank you for your love and support, and I hope you'll accompany me on this journey for a long time to come!

01 | ELIJAH

Trying to summon a demon in the middle of my bedroom probably hadn't been a good idea.

I was known for being an exemplary student. This didn't suit my MO. But I was curious. And when I was curious... things happened.

Like that time I'd been *sure* the cat hanging off my windowsill had talked to me. I'd managed to rescue her and set her free, and I knew she'd said *thank you* before leaving, even if no one believed me.

So yeah, summoning a demon might not have been a good idea, but I was going to try it anyway. If nothing else, it'd help me escape the boredom of this lousy day.

I'd found the journal—five bucks said you could guess where—tucked into a corner in the self-help section of the college library. *Can't finish your homework on time? Summon a demon to do it for you!*

Well, it didn't actually say that. Everything inside was hand-written in a barely legible scrawl. I'd had the journal for a week now, and I'd finally managed to read all of it. All twenty-five pages.

I'd copied over the *spell* for summoning a demon so I wouldn't make any mistakes. I'd also drawn a salt circle on my bedroom floor to keep the demon contained until I could make him my slave. Ha! If only...

I wanted to see what, if anything, would happen. I had no illusions about demons actually being real, but I had a feeling *something* would happen. And if it didn't? Well, I'd had a lifetime of disappointments. What was one more?

"All right, then. Let's do this," I mumbled to myself, pushing my hair away from my eyes as I pulled the paper closer to me.

The spell was in Latin, and though I'd translated it to English for my convenience, I planned on using the original version today. Words held power, or so the journal said.

I mumbled the first few words to myself to get into the groove, so to speak. Clearing my throat, I trained my eyes on the original spell, took a deep breath, and began chanting.

I didn't know what I'd expected to happen. Probably nothing. Demons didn't really exist after all. Right?

But the moment I finished the first stanza, the air thickened around me. It warmed and crackled, like a volcano was about to burst under my feet, and it was warning me to get the fuck away.

I took a deep breath and tried to swallow the next stanza, to not utter the words that talked about bringing forth a soul from the world below. But the words kept coming, as if now that they'd found an outlet, they *had to be* spoken.

Fuck. This was bad. Really, really bad. Somewhere in the world, I was sure there was a saying about the consequences of getting involved in something you didn't actually understand.

Sweat beaded on my forehead as the air turned hotter. A drop of moisture trickled down my spine, the only movement other than my lips, which still uttered the words, speaking Latin more fluently than I ever would've been able to on my own.

Finally, the spell ended, and I sucked in a large breath, dropping the paper and watching as it fluttered to the floor.

The same floor that shuddered a moment later as steam billowed out of it, as a huge fucking hole appeared in the middle of my bedroom, in the center of the salt circle.

I bet if I peeked into the hole, I wouldn't spot Mrs. Bailey watching TV with her dogs.

I shifted back, my eyes trained on the hole, really wishing it was a different kind that held my attention so completely, before waving the thought away.

After a wait that seemed to last forever, a figure rose from the fissure. And then he rose some more, and more until he was all the way out. Holy fuck, that was a huge guy.

He was also completely naked. His huge-ass schlong was right there, dangling in front of me as if he had no shame whatsoever. Eh, he probably didn't.

"Who dared summon Azazel from his slumber?" he bellowed toward my ceiling, and I realized the top of his head was barely a foot away from it. Fuck, he was enormous.

His skin was dark and shone like obsidian. Yes, I do mean his skin was literally black in color, like he'd rubbed charcoal all over himself before showing up here. (His... erm... privates told me that was actually his skin color and not a scrub gone wrong.)

When he turned to look at me, I almost swallowed my tongue. His eyes were red, and they *glowed*. Like he had tiny

LED lights behind his irises. I gave him a finger wave as more sweat slid down my forehead.

His brows furrowed, confusion replacing the fury. "Little mortal. Are you the one who summoned me?"

Little mortal? *Little mortal?* I was 6'1" and not small by any means, thank you very much.

I narrowed my eyes at him as I got to my feet. I died a little inside when I realized I barely reached his nipples at my full height. Still, I rallied myself and spoke in an even tone. "I'm not little. And yes, I summoned you. From what I understand, you'll now follow my orders for the next year if you wish to stay. Or you can return now if you'd rather go back to your world of doom and gloom."

"Doom and gloom? No, sir. My world has many pleasures you mortals know nothing about," the demon said with a huff, his hands twitching at his sides.

"Do you have arcades?" I demanded, raising a brow. "Video games? Movie theaters? *Internet?*"

Mr. Demon's—had he said his name was Azazel? Because that was a wicked title—eyes widened, and he tilted his head curiously. "Don't think we do. We have torture chambers, whores, mead. Oh, and gambling," he added as an afterthought, his eyes narrowing slightly.

I wrinkled my nose, shaking my head. "Oh no, that's awful. You need to see what real fun is. Be my slave and I'll show you everything."

What the fuck am I doing? This was crazy. I was talking to a literal demon. Why was I trying to convince him to stay? Was I really that lonely? Or maybe because I was so bad at making human friends, I'd decided a demon would be the next best thing. I might be going crazy. The jury was still out on that.

He eyed the journal at my feet and pointed at it. "Is that where you found the spell to summon me?"

I nodded, and how the fuck could someone with glowing red eyes give you *puppy-dog eyes?* Because this guy managed to do it just fine.

"May I see it, please?" he asked, extending a hand.

A demon being polite? I was immediately on guard.

"What, so you can figure out how to escape this circle I created? Yeah, I might be new to this, but I'm not a fool."

The puppy-dog eyes disappeared, and he raised a brow at me, a slight smirk gracing his surprisingly pink lips.

He leaned closer to me, his eyes holding on to mine and keeping me captive, and then he looked down and... blew out a puff of air. He broke the salt circle like it was child's play and met my eyes again, a feral grin spreading across his lips.

Well, *fuck.*

I leaped for the can of salt I'd placed on my desk, and Azazel gave a low chuckle.

"Chill, Monsieur. That ain't gonna work."

I cringed at the convoluted sentence as I looked back at him, only to freeze when I realized he wasn't in the circle anymore.

Instead, he'd taken a seat on my bed, his legs crossed at the ankles, his bits as visible as ever. *His naked ass is on my bedsheet,* I realized with growing horror, but I didn't know what to do. I was just glad my bed hadn't cracked under the guy's enormous weight.

Alexa, how do you get a demon to remove his posterior from your bed without angering him?

"I will be your servant, little mortal. For one year, no more. It's been a long time since I came to the mortal realm, and this should be entertaining. I've been feeling a mite bored recently."

Oh, do I feel you on that one, buddy, I thought wryly.

"Happy to hear that's not just a human trait. Feeling bored, I mean. Okay, then, we have a deal. One year of servitude, and I'll do my best to introduce you to the pleasures of the mortal realm during that time."

As I spoke, the fissure slowly disappeared, and I realized the sulfuric smell I'd credited to the hole was in fact emanating from my new servant. Of course it was. Why would my life ever be easy? Hell, I'd take manageable over the complete fuck-up it was most days.

"Okay, Azazel. My first order for you is: Go get a shower. You stink."

Azazel tilted his head again, giving me that same curious look, and asked, "What's a shower?"

Holy fucking jeebus.

"You don't know? Please tell me you're joking," I said, crossing my fingers behind my back.

"I'm joking," he told me, straight-faced and without inflection.

"Do you mean that?"

"No? I don't know what a shower is, dude," he said with a roll of his eyes, as if I was being difficult.

"How do you know what *dude* means and not know what a shower is?" I demanded, and he shrugged, blinking his red, glowy eyes.

"Oh for fuck's sake, come with me," I grumbled, resigned to the task.

"Now *fuck* I know," he declared, his voice hitching from what I hoped wasn't arousal, because I didn't know how I'd handle *that.* Ignoring him, I merely rolled my eyes as I led him to the bathroom. Well, *led* might not be the correct word since it literally took him three steps to get across my room. Then

I realized he wouldn't fit through the doorway. Even ducking might not be enough. Yeah, he was that tall.

"You should crawl," I told him, and he raised his brows at me with a horrified look, as if such a task was beneath him.

"You expect the great mighty Azazel to *crawl?*"

"Well, I could always order you to do it, couldn't I?" I mused out loud, and he huffed before maneuvering himself into the bathroom *without* crawling. I was almost tempted to clap and praise his flexibility. I was also tempted *by* his flexibility. Hmmm...

He couldn't even stand inside the bathroom; that's how tall he was. Before he broke my showerhead, I directed him to sit on the floor, and he promptly followed my direction, sitting cross-legged and looking at me expectantly.

"Okay, now I will show you the wonders of warm water and a detachable showerhead," I told him, and the demon appeared almost excited by the prospect.

Until I positioned the showerhead over his head and doused his golden hair—oh, did I mention he had unusually bright golden hair? The short, thick hair curled every which way, and it looked kinda pretty—with a warm spray of water. The shriek he let out would've rivaled my aunt Ruth's, and let me tell you, that woman could reach a pitch so high only the dogs could hear her at one point.

"Shut up! It's just water!"

As if realizing what he'd done, he glared at me and shook his head. "I'm a strong, manly demon, and that sound did not originate from my mouth," he said firmly, as if telling me that was all it would take for me to believe him.

I rolled my eyes as I cleaned him, appreciating the warm, smooth skin of his shoulders. I probably shouldn't be touching him. Actually, I should've just told him how it worked and left him to it.

His dick was right there, though, and it was pointing *right at me.* Of course, it was too big for me, but there were ways I could have fun with it, couldn't I?

What the fuck are you thinking, Eli? He's a demon. *He's your* servant. *No sexy thoughts about the overly large fantasy creature. Especially when he can't say no to you.*

"How much longer will you torture me, Master Little Mortal?" Azazel whined, and I tsked.

"My name's Elijah. And I won't stop unless you promise not to call me little mortal anymore."

Azazel grunted, but nodded grudgingly, and I turned off the shower. The water on the floor had an oily sheen to it, and even without using soap, Azazel looked—and smelled—much cleaner. I didn't think he was ready for the horrors of fragrant body wash yet, so I'd let him escape today.

One step at a time.

Next, I needed to figure out just what the fuck I had gotten myself into. Curiosity *would not* kill this particular cat. I didn't survive everything my father put me through and all the bullies to be taken down by a mythical creature, no sir.

The game was on.

02 | ELIJAH

"How tall are you anyway?" I asked as I hunted through my closet for something that would cover up the massive demon who *again* had his butt planted firmly on my bedsheet. It was looking more and more like the bedsheet would be my only option. He *would* look pretty cool in a toga.

"Hmmm... 8'2", I think? I was 8'6" before they chopped off my horns," Azazel said, and I dropped the shirt I'd been looking at and turned to look at him, eyes wide.

"They chopped off your horns? Why?" I demanded, stepping closer to him and also wondering who *they* were, exactly. The other demons, maybe? I couldn't even see the top of his head, so if there were horn stubs up there, I didn't know. I hadn't felt them when I was giving him a shower, but then again, I might've been a tiny bit distracted by his golden hair.

Azazel sniffed, glancing away from me. For the first time since he'd arrived, I saw something more in him than an arrogant demon. It made me wonder if the way he acted was really him, or just a persona he'd been trained to put on. "Because, according to them, I wasn't fierce and demonic enough."

Huh. If this demon wasn't fierce, what did the fiercer ones look like? And why did I feel bad for this guy?

I guess because I knew what being the *weak one* felt like.

"Eh, you look demonic enough to me. Now, I don't have clothes your size, so you'll have to cover up with the sheet while I do some shopping. Hell, I don't even know if I'll find anything in your size," I grumbled as I eyed his massive frame, simply to figure out what sizes I'd need to look for, obviously.

Azazel's gaze was stuck on me as water dripped from his hair. Fuck, he was going to soak my bed if he hadn't already.

Grabbing a towel, I climbed up onto the bed and walked over to stand behind him. Now I could see there were half-an-inch long stumps where they would've been, peeking through the strands of his hair. Poor guy.

I covered his head with the towel and started wiping, humming under my breath. From the few memories I had of my mom, the ones of her drying my hair and humming a song were my favorite. They were full of calm and comfort, and whenever I was too close to a panic attack, that was the memory I returned to.

"What—What are you doing?" Azazel asked hesitantly, and I smiled.

"I'm wiping your hair so you don't get my bed wet."

"Hmmm..." Azazel hummed. "Clothes? You mean the garments you cover yourself with?"

"Yep. If someone sees you, you don't wanna give them an eyeful, you know? Human etiquette."

"I'm not human," he pointed out, and I scoffed.

"Trust me, I know that. But you're in the human world, so you gotta follow the human rules," I explained, though him being naked was the least of my problems when it came to taking him out into the public. He'd create mass panic if he went out there with red eyes and his eight-foot-tall frame. He was like a Hulk dipped in ink and wearing Thor's hair. Huh. Maybe I could pass it off as a weird, Comic-Con thing.

"Okay," Azazel said, and the air thickened for a moment the same way it had before he'd shown up, but it was less intense this time. When it was normal again, I blinked stupidly as I realized he was wearing human clothes. Actually, he was wearing clothes exactly identical to my outfit: gray sweatpants and an old, white t-shirt.

"Well... that's one thing taken care of. I don't think you can blend in with this height. Can you shorten yourself?" I asked as I climbed down the bed and put the towel in the bathroom to dry before returning to the bedroom.

"I will not lower myself to the size of puny humans like you," Azazel growled, and I narrowed my eyes at him, placing my hands on my hips.

"People will scream if they see you right now," I said, and his eyes widened.

"You...you think I'm ugly? So ugly people would scream in disgust if they saw me?" Azazel asked, and I really wasn't sure if he was pulling my leg or if I'd really hurt him.

"I meant your size, you big goof. Humans don't grow that tall," I explained, and he nodded.

The air went all warm and tingly again, and then Azazel was a nice, human-sized demon sitting on my bed, wearing clothes that looked just like mine.

When I'd decided to try summoning a demon, I'd never, ever expected it to actually work. But now that Azazel was here, I didn't know what to do with that, and he was going to be staying here for a whole freaking year.

The alarm on my phone went off, reminding me it would be time for my classes soon. Fuck. Why had I done this on a school day? And before class at that?

"What is that thing? Shall I smite it?" Azazel asked, and I looked up to find his eyes trained on my phone.

"Oh no, no touching my phone!"

"Oh, is that a phone? I've heard of it from the other demons. Humans love those things, don't they?"

"Um, yeah," I said, rolling my eyes. "Phones keep you connected to the whole world. Life would be painful without the internet."

He gave my phone a thoughtful look and thankfully refrained from smiting it. "So!" I said, as I walked over to my closet and hunted down an outfit for myself. "I need to get to class. Why don't you wait here until I get back?"

"I shall come with you. You promised to show me the human world," he said plainly, and I glanced back at him, a t-shirt thrown over my shoulder and a pair of underwear in my hand.

"I promised to show you the fun side of it, and trust me, classes are *not* fun," I assured him before returning to my hunt for a clean pair of jeans.

"What are classes?" Azazel asked, tilting his head to the side.

"Class? It's where we learn new things, or the same old boring things, so we can later get a job and earn money."

"Hmmm...I wish to learn more about humans. I shall join you."

I narrowed my eyes at him. Even though he was human-sized in appearance now, he still had an unearthly feel to him. Anyone who saw him would do a double take. Not to mention his eyes were still ruby red.

"If people saw you, they'd stare. I don't like it when people stare," I admitted. I didn't want to say people would be freaked out if they saw him, since I'd already done that and almost hurt his feelings once.

Why did I care about the emotions of this demon anyway? Because he hadn't done anything truly demonic since he came here? Or because I felt a strange kinship to this demon I didn't fully understand?

"They won't stare, I assure you, Li—I mean, human master."

"Call me Elijah, please. Are you going to turn invisible?"

He shook his head, making me frown. How would he avoid the stares then?

"Trust me, Elijah." I shivered at the way my name sounded on his lips. Surprised at my own reaction, I quickly escaped to the bathroom and changed into the jeans, t-shirt, and hoodie I'd picked out.

When I stepped back into the bedroom, I found Azazel waiting just where I'd left him.

"Shall I change my clothes to what you're wearing?" he asked as he took in my clothing, and I shook my head.

I picked out another outfit for him, and he used his magic to replicate it on his skin, as if changing like humans do would've been too much trouble. I was pretty sure my clothes would've fit him in this form, even if he was a little bulkier than me.

My phone buzzed with another alarm, reminding me I'd be late if I didn't leave *now*.

I took a deep breath and glanced at the demon I'd summoned because I was bored. Well, that was one way to cure monotony.

"Come on, Azazel. Time to go."

03 | AZAZEL

Humans were such dull creatures.

I blew out a sigh as I watched my little human sit there and listen to the other human talk. The older human was droning on and on about something called coding or debugging or some other boring human computer thing, and if his voice wasn't so horribly scratchy, I'd have fallen asleep.

It had been around 500 years since someone summoned me to the human realm. The woman who'd summoned me then had been a powerful witch. She'd needed all her magic to summon me, and yet this measly human with no magic had somehow accomplished the same. Not only that, he'd also formed a bond with me.

Unlike what the little human thought, I didn't need to be summoned to be able to visit the human realm. I could travel whenever I wished, and I had done so many times in the past.

The only annoyance was that without a bond with someone in the human realm, I couldn't have a corporeal form. I could watch, observe, learn, but I couldn't talk, touch, or do anything to anyone, which sucked all the fun out of things. It was why I'd allowed the little human to form the bond in the first place. I was tired of watching from the shadows. Yet, there I was, doing the same again because the human needed to listen to the droning man at the front. Just how long could someone talk about computers?

The little human wasn't anything special, though he was pretty to look at. He had copper curls that framed his pale face and golden wire-rimmed round glasses too big for his eyes. He was suitably tall for a human, but tiny compared to me.

There was something about him, though. Something that told me I could trust him, that I didn't have to put on the show I'd been putting on for him. That I could be myself around him. I didn't know if I could trust this instinct, if I could trust Elijah. My summoners were almost never good people. Anyone who ever summoned a demon had plans, big, world-dominating plans that they forced us to help them with. So far, Elijah hadn't told me about any such proposals. Hell, the only real order he'd given me was to take a shower, and even that hadn't truly been phrased as an order.

Unless he was just waiting for me to let my guard down, and then when I'd finally accepted he had no evil plans, he would drop them on me. Unfortunately, it'd happened before, so I wasn't just imagining shit.

A bell rang somewhere, and the humans all stood up as the droning man finally, finally, ended his monologue. I knew he was a professor, and I knew he'd been teaching, but to me all he was was an annoyance standing between me and the little human's promise to show me the "fun" parts of the human realm. He didn't know that I'd already seen most of them, and I wasn't going to tell him. I wanted to see what he'd do, where he'd take me. I wanted to know if my instincts were right, or if he was just too good of an actor.

I stepped out of the shadows, making some girl squeak as she stepped away from me, and headed toward the front.

"Lit—" He raised a brow at me, and I growled under my breath. "Elijah," I forced out through gritted teeth. "Now that you're done torturing me, how about you hold up your end of the deal and get us out of this hell?"

He blinked up at me as he put his laptop back in his bag, his face a picture of innocence. He might fool a human with that face, but not me. He'd summoned a demon like me without the use of magic, simply with his willpower. He was crafty and dangerous, especially with an angelic face.

"Oh, we aren't done yet. I have two more classes to attend before I'll be free."

My eyes widened at the horror of spending another two hours in that torturous situation, and I barely stopped myself from whimpering. "If that is so, I will return in two hours."

"Where will you go?" he asked as he slung his bag across his shoulder and stood up. I followed him out of the room, ignoring the people who watched us with gaping mouths. I was in my human form, so I didn't know what they found so fascinating about me, and I couldn't care less.

"Anywhere but where you're headed," I told him, and he chuckled.

"All right, I won't torture you. But you promise you'll come back?" His voice was softer when he asked the question, and I took a moment to read his aura, an ability that had helped me avoid a lot of punishments over the years. Afraid. Nervous. Lonely.

Lonely? Why was he lonely? He seemed like a well-adjusted, friendly human, if a bit sassy. Granted, I'd known him for only a few hours, but he didn't seem like the kind of person who would be lacking in company.

"I promise," I answered gruffly, not wanting him to sense that I wasn't completely opposed to the idea of spending time with him.

"See you in two hours, then," he murmured softly, and I let him walk off, slipping into another bit of shadow when no one was watching. Taking my incorporeal form, I found myself following Elijah instead of going off on my own.

A male human the same age as Elijah whispered something to his female companion, both of their eyes on Elijah, their mouths twisted in disgust. I narrowed my eyes at them as I shifted closer to my human. I wondered what the story was there.

As I followed Elijah, I realized that every human of his age had one of two reactions when they saw him. They either intentionally ignored him, or they treated him like he was a pariah, eyeing him with barely restrained disgust.

Just what was Elijah's story? Had he really done something evil to earn their ire? Or were they just being judgy and punishing him for something that wasn't his fault?

At least now I knew why he was lonely. This new layer of mystery certainly made Elijah more interesting.

A human with no friends and a willpower strong enough to summon a demon like me. There was something special about Little Human Elijah, and I would find out what it was, even if I had to suffer through two hours of torture with him.

With a snap of my fingers, I made sure all the boring, human details would work themselves out. Then, I took my corporeal human form and walked into Elijah's classroom like I belonged there, which I now did.

I slid into the empty seat beside Elijah and turned to him with a smile. I offered him my hand and grinned at him as he gave me a puzzled look. "Hello, I'm Az. It's nice to meet you."

"What are you doing here?" he hissed at me, though he shook my hand.

"What do you mean?" I asked, tilting my head. "I'm a new student. Won't you introduce yourself?"

Elijah stared at me, open-mouthed, and I winked at him as the other humans murmured behind us, buzzing like little bees that I'd have thoroughly enjoyed crushing if I wasn't afraid of incurring the wrath of the Otherworlders.

The professor walked into the room, and I leaned into Elijah, speaking softly. "Buckle up, Little Human. The torture begins now."

04 | AZAZEL

SOMEONE, ANYONE, SAVE ME! Save me from this agony! I'm losing my will to live with every second that goes by!

"Will you stop fucking sighing?" Elijah snapped, his voice low, and I glared at him.

"How can you enjoy this drivel? Are you a masochist, perhaps? Because that would certainly explain things!" I growled under my breath, tempted to kick him under the desk. I was above such juvenile gestures, though, so I resorted to just glaring at him and sighing yet again.

"I'm not, trust me. And this *drivel* is important if I want to get an education and find a job so I can pay back my student loans," Elijah whispered, and I narrowed my eyes as I tried to make sense of that.

"So, wait. You pay money to someone, money that you don't actually have, to learn this drivel. Then, you use what you learn to earn money to pay back the money you spent to learn in in the first place? How does that make any sense?" I demanded. Humans really were a stupid species. Either that or they knew something the rest of us didn't. Surely, there was a better way to have a good life?

Elijah buried his face in his palms, groaning softly. After a moment, he glanced up at me, and he looked... tired. "Can we please just focus? I know none of this matters to you, and I know what I promised you, and I'll keep my bargain. But this is important to me. Please?"

I huffed out a breath, mildly disgusted with myself that I found his pleading eyes melting my resolve. Without giving him a reply, I turned to the front and entertained myself with the idea of turning the professor into a mouse. The one with fur, not the one that went click-click.

The bell rang again, and Elijah turned to me. "It's lunchtime. Last class is after lunch. Can you eat human food?" he asked, tilting his head to the side so his curls fell into his eyes.

My mouth watered as I realized I'd get to eat human food again. I'd missed the variety and spices and all that deliciousness. One of the reasons I'd limited my visits to the human realm was that I hated looking at human food and not being able to eat it, but it would be different this time.

"By the drool dripping out of your mouth, I'm going to take a guess and say you like human food," Elijah said, and I wiped my mouth hastily. It was dry, but the gesture did make him chuckle.

"Where's the food?" I asked. There would be no dilly-dallying. I couldn't believe I hadn't gone looking for food the moment we settled our contract.

Elijah took me to a large room he called the cafeteria, and I breathed in the scent of chicken, spices, chocolate, and coffee.

"You should get the food for me," I told Elijah, and he looked up at me with a raised brow, his glasses following it up.

"I thought I was the boss here."

I rolled my eyes at him before turning around to eye all the food. "I don't know what most of these dishes are called, and I'm tempted to get some of each. I suppose you won't be able to pay for that," I said. It wasn't the whole truth. I wasn't as clueless about the human realm as I acted, but I'd learned from experience that it was better to let your summoner underestimate you. That way, they usually didn't ask you to do something too horrible.

Elijah's eyes widened, and he hurried over to the counter, making his food request as I grinned at his back, settling comfortably against a wall as I waited for him.

Once we had our food, Elijah led me to a table in the far corner, away from the other kids. Well, they weren't really kids. They were all in their twenties, including Elijah. But to someone as old as me, they were nothing more than children.

I took a huge bite of my burger, humming at the taste, as Elijah popped his soda can. I took my time relishing the various tastes, from the creamy mayo to the tangy sauce and everything in between.

"Why does everyone dislike you?" I asked as Elijah took a sip of his soda, and he made a weird, choking sound before he started coughing.

I watched him with furrowed brows, wondering what he was doing, and it took me a moment to realize he was actually in pain. I patted his back—a little roughly, I supposed—and he almost face-planted into his food, catching himself just in time.

"What the fuck, Az? New rule: don't pop questions at me when I'm eating or drinking," Elijah growled out, and I patted the top of his head like he was my dog.

"It's okay. You're not dead," I told him in case he hadn't realized, and he rolled his eyes at me.

He went back to eating, waving at my plate to get me to do the same. His eyes were far away as he ate, and I gobbled up my food as he slowly nibbled at his.

When I was all done, he offered me his leftovers—which was basically all of his food minus one bite of pasta and the can of soda. I wasn't about to say no to good food, though, so I ate it all just in time for the bell to announce it was time for some more torture.

I followed Elijah into the new class, taking the seat beside him as the professor walked into the class and started her hour of boredom.

Elijah listened to the woman with interest while I watched *him* with even greater interest. Whether the choking on soda had been intended or not, I knew he'd intentionally eluded my question. Elijah was hiding something, and if there was one thing I knew as a demon, it was how to break someone to make them reveal all their secrets.

The only problem was I didn't *want* to break Elijah. I wanted him to willingly tell me, to show me all that hurt he was hiding beneath his snark, his I-don't-care attitude and the loneliness that seemed to be a permanent part of his aura.

I will figure you out, little human. One way or another.

05 | ELIJAH

Azazel was acting weird. I mean, he was already pretty strange, but the way he kept shooting me these glances throughout the class made me wonder what he was cooking up in that demonic brain of his.

I hadn't expected him to join the class as a fucking student of all things, and I had absolutely no idea what he was planning. All I knew was that whatever it was, it would annoy the hell out of me.

I didn't even know why I'd thought summoning a fucking demon would be a good idea. No, that's not true. I hadn't thought it would be a good idea because I hadn't expected it to fucking work. But here I was, bonded to a massive, dark, and handsome demon for the next year.

Wait, *handsome*? I shook my head, eyeing him out of the corner of my eyes.

If he'd heard what the other students murmured about me when they thought I couldn't hear, his curiosity made sense. After all, he'd asked me point blank what I'd done to piss off the others, and while I'd managed to deflect the question with my impromptu choking act, I knew he was still wondering, and I had a feeling he wasn't going to let my avoidance of the topic deter him.

The fact of the matter was I hadn't done a thing. Not that that mattered to anyone.

Once the class was done, Azazel and I returned home. I rented a small apartment just outside of campus—since my dorm mates had made my life hell after everything blew up, forcing me to move out and scrape together what money I had to get this place—and while it didn't feel like home yet, it was all I needed for now.

I threw my messenger bag onto a chair and grabbed a water bottle, drinking it all as Azazel lurked like a dark shadow behind me.

When I turned around, he was back in his real form, his clothes having increased in size to accommodate him. The top of his head was inches away from the ceiling, and I waved at him to get seated before he scratched it up and caused me my deposit.

"Why did you change sizes?" I asked curiously as he settled on the floor, crossing his legs and looking completely at ease.

"You try squeezing yourself three times smaller and tell me how it feels," he growled, and I rolled my eyes. He hadn't squeezed himself *three* times smaller. Maybe one. One and a half, tops.

Remembering my promise to him, I stretched, hoping we'd be back in time for me to start on some of my assignments. My schoolwork was one of the few things in my life I still had control over, and the last thing I needed was to mess that up.

"All right, I promised to show you around. You'll have to change sizes to go outside, though," I reminded him, and he grumbled in annoyance, but did.

"Where are we going?"

It wasn't late enough to visit a club, not that I wanted to go to one, but maybe I could take him somewhere else fun.

"The arcade."

Azazel's eyes widened at my answer, and he actually looked excited. "Oh! I would like that very much!"

"You know what an arcade is?" I asked, a touch skeptical, and he rolled his eyes.

"I'm not completely clueless, human," he said, and I shrugged. His knowledge of the human world was so random it made me wonder exactly where he'd learned what he knew, but I hadn't asked. I was also curious about his world and what it looked like. He'd mentioned whores, mead, and gambling when he showed up, and I wondered if that meant he really did live in Hell.

"Okay. Can you take us there, or do we need to call a cab?" I asked, hoping we wouldn't have to. While I had enough savings to last for a while if I was careful, I didn't want to waste any money, and if this demon could help me avoid some expenses, then at least summoning him wouldn't have been completely useless.

Azazel rolled his eyes again—he really needed to stop doing that—and didn't answer. Instead, I felt his magic stir around us, a little more familiar now, and in the next moment, we were in a dark alley, the sound of the evening crowd drifting through the opening.

"Whoa," I exclaimed, feeling just a little woozy and disoriented.

"Come on. What are you waiting for?" Az demanded, annoyance prickling at his tone.

"Yeah, yeah," I mumbled, following after him.

The arcade had been there for as long as I'd lived in this town, and I visited it a lot, not just because I liked the games, but because people usually left you alone. Everyone was focused on their games and the people they were there with, and for a few hours, I could just enjoy being around people without having their attention on me.

"Fucking hell," Az murmured, amazement in his tone as he looked around at all the bright, flashy lights, loud music and cheers echoing around the room.

"Can you magic up some tokens, or do I need to pay?" I asked, wondering what the limits of his magic were.

"You really need to stop asking me stupid questions and just tell me what you want me to do," he said, and I sighed.

"Okay, grumpy-pants. See that kid's hand?" I said, pointing at a teenager who was stuffing a token into the claw machine. "Make me twenty of those."

Azazel held out his palm to me, and I watched as it filled with tokens, shaking my head in wonder. He offered them to me, and I took two before pushing the rest back to him.

"They're for you," I said, and he looked like I'd given him the moon. Grinning widely, he turned to head deeper into the room before glancing back at me, as if waiting for my permission.

"Go have fun, Az. Find me when you're done." His grin widened, and off he went to play, looking everything like an excited kid and nothing like the dangerous demon he was supposed to be.

I glanced at the two tokens in my hand and then over to the claw machine. I'd never won anything on that stupid thing before.

"Oh, what the hell," I muttered and headed toward it.

"Are you done?" I asked for the thousandth time, feeling extra prickly because the claw machine had yet again defeated me, and just like every other time, Azazel waved me off.

Of all the games he could've been hooked on, he'd chosen Pac-Man. I mean, sure it was a classic, but it'd been *three hours*. I was exhausted, and I needed to get back home and start working on my assignment, not to mention I was fucking hungry.

Food. That's it!

"I'll be right back," I said, and he barely gave me a second glance as I walked off toward the fast food counter. I placed an order for their cheesiest burger and biggest bucket of fries, taking it back to Az once I'd paid.

"Hey, I'll be over there eating. Shout when you need me to feed it more coins," I said, and Azazel's eyes locked onto the burger, his lips parting. I had the sudden urge to lean closer and check if demon lips tasted different than human ones, and I jerked back, shaking off the errant thought.

"I'm done," he declared as he stood up, and I bit back a smile as I waved him toward the seating area.

I tore the burger into two, handing him the bigger part before demolishing mine. I hadn't felt like eating in the cafeteria earlier with the student body buzzing with chatter because someone had decided to sit with me, and I was ravenous.

Az watched me eat with a contemplative look in his eyes, and I raised a brow at him. He merely winked at me before taking a big bite, moaning indecently and not very quietly either. I glared at him, and he shrugged.

Once we'd eaten, Azazel looked like he wanted to go back to the game, but I shook my head and pointed to the door. He gave me a look tiny puppies would be jealous of, but I knew better than to let him get away with it.

Just before we reached the exit, he stopped me and raised his index finger before heading back the way we'd come, and I followed him in case he got hooked to the game again.

I stopped short when I realized he was at the claw machine and watched as he expertly picked up the largest stuffed toy—a penguin wearing a pilot's goggles—and deposited it at the exit slide. He had to have used his magic to do that. Right?

He hurried back to me once he had it and offered the penguin to me. I took it with a raised brow and couldn't help petting its soft head.

"Thank you for bringing me here. I had fun," Azazel said, a sincere smile on his face, and I nodded, my fingers tightening around the stuffed toy.

When we got home, I placed the stuffed toy on my bed, then felt silly about it and put it into my closet. Then, just before I went to bed—Az had returned to his realm to sleep, with the orders to be back in time for class—I pulled it back out and stuck it beside my pillow, annoyed at how attached I'd become to the stupid thing.

06 | ELIJAH

It'd been a few weeks since I summoned Az, and we'd fallen into something of a routine, starting with a hearty, magical—literally—breakfast that was from a different cuisine every day, then classes after that, with lunch in the cafeteria. In the evening, we went out, sometime to the park, others to the clubs, the arcade, and one time, we even went to the library, and I was surprised to realize I actually enjoyed hanging out with Azazel. The fact that I hadn't had to spend a single dollar since he got here was also a bonus.

Tonight, we hadn't gone anywhere because I had a few projects due on Monday, and I was behind. Az had offered to do them for me, but I didn't want to cheat my way through school.

There wasn't much space in my one room—kitchen combined—one-bedroom apartment, and you could hear everything from anywhere in the apartment, which was why when everything went extremely quiet a few minutes later, I felt that it was well within my rights to be suspicious.

I stopped typing and cocked my ear for any sound I could catch from the bedroom. I'd shooed him there when his presence in the living room had become too distracting, but now I was regretting my decision. Was he going through my things? He'd grown more and more curious about my past over the weeks, and I wouldn't put it past him to be looking through my things for clues. I'd have heard it if he was, right?

There. Murmuring. As if Az was talking to someone. But who?

Slowly, I tiptoed to the bedroom doorway, glad he'd left the door open.

I peeked inside and my eyes widened at the sight before me. Azazel sat on the floor in his true form, and on his lap was a huge, black... dog with red eyes just like his and a wide, doggy grin. The tips of its ears were burning, or at least they looked like they had red flames licking at them, though I supposed the dog wouldn't look so happy if it hurt.

That wasn't even the question, though. The question was—what the hell was this... this *hellhound* doing in my bedroom?

I opened my mouth to ask that very question, but I must've made some sound because both Azazel and the dog looked up at me.

Before I could do anything more than give the dog a wide-eyed look, it lunged, tackling me to the living room floor.

Fuck.

"Holy crap on a—" I snapped my mouth shut before the hound could stick its tongue inside, trying and failing to scramble away from it as it licked my face, its drool clinging to my skin.

Azazel, the asshole, was laughing, all his teeth on display as he watched us. I narrowed my eyes at him. "Get this mutt off me,"

I growled, and it looked like he was trying to resist the compulsion to obey my command—something he'd told me could be anywhere from uncomfortable to downright painful—before he huffed and gave a whistle, calling the mutt back to his side. I scrambled to my feet, dusting off the ink-black fur it'd covered me with and wiping my face with the end of my t-shirt.

"Where did the fucking hellhound come from?" I demanded, and Az scrunched his nose at me. For an eight-foot-tall demon, he looked awfully adorable at that moment.

"She's not a hellhound. She's a demon hound," he corrected me, making me roll my eyes.

"Po-tah-to, po-tay-to," I grumbled, glaring at the mutt, who was drooling all over my bedroom floor now, her tail whipping like mad as she looked from me to Az and back, as if trying to decide which one of us she wanted to maul.

"Why is she here?"

"Hella missed me," he said simply, and I blinked at him.

"So wait. She's not a hellhound, but you named her Hella?" I demanded, flabbergasted.

"Hella isn't for hellhound," Azazel said, scoffing at me like I didn't know shit. "The time I was in the human realm before I got her, I heard a human call a puppy 'Hella cute.' I thought she was cute when I saw her, so I named her Hella."

I bit my lip as a chuckle threatened to slip through, but then I caught the earnest look on his face, and I couldn't hold it in. I started laughing. I laughed harder than I remembered doing in a long time, and my stomach had started to hurt by the time I managed to gasp out, "Oh my god, you're fucking adorable."

He gasped as if I'd just insulted him, patting Hella on the rump. Like she knew exactly what to do, she tackled me again. Thankfully, I was steadier on my feet this time, and managed to keep her from making me fall on my ass. It wasn't like she wasn't trying, though. She was a big dog, bigger than any breed we had here for sure.

"Is Hella going to stay with us?" I asked warily, and Az shook his head.

"She'll go back in a while. She was just visiting. She stays in the demon realm for the most part, and all of us take care of her. Her mom had been in the demon realm for a long time, and before she moved on, she brought Hella for us."

"She brought her for you?" I asked, and he nodded.

"Technically, Hella's dead, like me. Her mom brought her to us from the realm she was taken to after her death."

I blinked at the sudden influx of information, struggling to make sense of everything. Putting it on the backburner for now, I asked a different question instead.

"Could you go back to the demon realm if you wanted to? Like, would you be able to come back?"

"I can travel between the realms without a problem. If I'm not around and you need me, all you have to do is call my name, and I'll hear you wherever I am," Azazel answered, like he could see right through me and knew exactly why I'd been asking.

I nodded slowly, realizing Hella was kinda cute now that she wasn't trying to maul me. I'd never had a pet before, and even though I knew I couldn't keep her, I kinda wanted to.

"Alright, I need to get back to my project. Do you need to sleep?" I asked, and I was immediately reminded of his first night here when I'd asked him the same question.

He'd stared at me, one brow raised. "Of course I need to fucking sleep. I'm not a damn robot."

"You know what a robot is?" I'd asked curiously, and he'd rolled his eyes.

"I know everything," he'd said with a huff, and I'd given him an indulgent smile, finding that hard to believe after he'd asked me what a shower was.

"Sure you do. Okay, you probably won't fit on my couch, not even in your smaller form, but I have a sleeping bag you can take," I'd offered, and the disgusted look on his face had almost made me laugh.

"You... you want the great Azazel to sleep on the floor?" he'd asked, utterly horrified.

"You know, you should try being a little humble sometimes. And yes, I want you to sleep on the floor. I'm not giving you my bed."

Az had narrowed his eyes at me. "In my realm, I have a massive bed with silk sheets and more pillows than I could ever need. I shall return to my realm to sleep, and you can call on me when you go to school."

I'd contemplated the idea, and a part of me hadn't wanted to let him go, afraid he wouldn't return, but I'd put faith in our bond—and his fondness for human food—and agreed.

"In a bit, yes. I will return with Hella. You only have one class tomorrow, yes? I would like to stay a little longer, meet with my friends. You can call on me if you need me, and I'll be there," he said, and I agreed instantly, mostly because it would give me some extra time to complete my projects.

"Can I go to your realm?" I asked curiously, the question one of the many, many questions I had about him and his world, and he gave me a startled look.

"Humans aren't allowed to travel to other realms. Not unless..." he trailed off, shaking his head.

"Unless what?" I asked, curiosity even more piqued.

"Unless nothing, little human. Hella and I will have a cozy cuddle night in my big bed. See you tomorrow."

And the dog and the demon were gone.

I shook my head before returning to my desk, sighing as I reread the last paragraph I'd written before getting distracted. This was going to be a long, long night.

By the time I finally went to bed, I was closer to my wake up time than my bedtime. Still, I forced myself to sleep, not wanting to miss tomorrow's lecture because I fell asleep in class.

I didn't call Azazel back when I went to school the next morning, though I was tempted to, despite the fact that he was annoying when he was bored, and I really needed to focus on my studies. Not to mention I didn't want him listening to all the gossip that followed me and ask questions I'd rather not answer, though I was sure he'd done that all this time. He hadn't asked me about anything he'd heard, though, for which I was grateful.

After I finished my class, I'd call him, and we would hang out. Maybe I could take him to the planetarium today. Would that be something he'd enjoy?

"Yo, psycho, where's the new kid?" I stopped short as Louis stepped into my path, blocking my way. He was an oversized gym junkie, and while I'd seen him around, I'd managed to avoid a confrontation. It seemed like my luck had run out.

I glared at him. There weren't many people taller than me, but he was just an inch or two taller. Not enough that I needed to raise my head to look at him, but enough that he felt he could loom over me.

"Why the fuck would I know?" I growled as two of his friends stepped close on either side of him.

Louis narrowed his eyes and stepped closer, breathing in my space as he watched me. "He has been around you since the day he joined, and now he isn't here. For all we know, you have him tied up at your place, waiting for you to cut him."

A sharp pain lanced through my chest, my gut twisting at his words, but I forced myself not to show it on my face. "Maybe I have him tied up and waiting for me to fuck him. What's it matter to you?"

His face screwed up into a scowl, and he pushed me back hard. I stumbled, righting myself before I fell on my ass.

"You fucking sicko. Did you kill him? I told them you were dangerous. Evil breeds evil, doesn't it?"

Knowing what was coming from experience, I regretted not calling Azazel back. Fuck, this was going to hurt.

07 | AZAZEL

WHY DID I HAVE to be stuck with such a careless, stupid human? What was the point of summoning a demon if you never made him work for you?

I watched as the lump of muscles punched my human in the jaw, making his glasses fall off as he stumbled back. I was glad I'd left the demon realm earlier than I'd been planning to and gone looking. I would've hated to miss out on this. How long did I need to wait for him to learn his lesson before stepping in? How breakable were humans?

I leaned back against the wall, deciding I'd give my human one more chance to call me before I stepped in. But the moment the asshole punched Elijah in the stomach and made him cry out in pain, an anger the likes of which I'd never felt before coursed through me.

I changed into my human form as I made myself visible and stalked toward the three assholes who'd decided to gang up on my little human.

I picked up his glasses and handed them to him, moving him so he leaned against the wall. Then I turned to the assholes and let loose.

I didn't spare the other two who'd just stood there, knowing if they'd been given the chance they wouldn't have hesitated in hurting him either. Within a minute, all three were on the floor, groaning and whimpering in pain like the sad sacks of blood and bones they were. I glared at them with narrowed eyes, sorely tempted to knock each of them out. Instead, I decided to leave them with a warning.

"If you ever dare to come near him, you won't have anything left worth whimpering about," I growled at them, letting just enough of my real eyes show to freak them out, before stepping back and turning to Elijah.

He gave me a hesitant smile, glasses back on his face. I could see he was shaken up, even if he'd never tell me, and I wondered what the assholes had meant about evil breeding evil. Had my little human's parents been evil? But why would he be punished for their crimes?

"Come, human," I said, pulling him into my arms as he gave a squeak.

"What are you—put me down!" he shrieked, his long limbs flailing in my hold.

"Hush. Let me carry you, my damsel in distress," I teased, and he chuckled as he rolled his eyes at me, relaxing a little and letting me hold him properly.

"I'm not a fucking damsel. I didn't ask you to save me."

"Why didn't you? I mean, what's the point of summoning a demon if you won't make him fight your battles?" I asked, honestly curious. I'd never been summoned for anything other than doing my master's bidding, but so far the only time Elijah had made me do something horrendous was when he made me shower. It didn't make sense to me.

"I didn't summon you to fight for me. And anyway, those assholes don't usually bother me. They must've had a bad day," he said, and I felt like he was forcing himself to make light of the whole thing, which annoyed me to no end.

"Why *did* you summon me?" I asked, using my magic to get us back to his home.

Elijah shrugged as I placed him on his bed, wincing as he touched his jaw, which had started to change color. Human bodies were so weird, and so weak too.

"Are you going to die?" I asked before he could answer my previous question, and he gave me a shocked look.

"What? No! No, I'm not. Why would you say that?" he demanded, his palm pressing against his chest, as if my words had physically hurt him. *So dramatic.*

"Humans are weak," I said with a shrug, and he rolled his pretty eyes.

Wait, *pretty*?!

"We aren't that weak. I'm not going to die. Probably can't kiss anyone for a while, but it's not like I *have* anyone to kiss," he said with a grin, before wincing and touching his jaw softly.

"Is *that* why you summoned me?" I teased, and his eyes widened, his cheeks reddened, but he didn't shake his head. At least, not instantly.

Huh. Did my little human *want* to kiss me?

"Shut up, you crazy demon. I summoned you because I was bored and lonely, and it felt like a good idea at the time. I don't need you to fight my battles for me, though I appreciate you coming to my rescue. I just want you to have fun and be your friend, hopefully."

He was such a strange human. I'd never met anyone like him. He'd summoned me, a demon with unimaginable power, and he'd never once asked me what I could do. Hell, he'd never ordered me to do anything except take that disgusting shower. Had he really just summoned me for something as simple as wanting company? Could I really have gotten lucky this time?

"I can be your friend. I'll be the best friend you've ever had, and I'll cut anyone who thinks they can hurt my new BFF," I promised him, doing my best to make my face look honest and earnest, and he gave me a wide-eyed look, as if regretting everything.

"Oh, boy," he muttered to himself as I grinned at him.

Biting my lip, I placed my palm on his cheek, startling him. I'd changed into my true form when we got home, and my palm covered the side of his face from his hairline to chin. Before he could ask what I was doing, I healed his jaw. While I usually needed orders from him to be able to use my magic, things like these were allowed since I could never hurt him by healing him, and I didn't think he knew he could ask me.

"Wow," he breathed, and I trailed my palm down his body to his stomach, pushing my magic into the place the second punch had landed. "Holy fuck."

"There. All good and new," I said, and Elijah chuckled.

"It seems like I got an impromptu day off. I really wanted to attend that lecture, though," he said on a sigh, and I remembered him saying how important those were to him.

"I can help. You just need to phrase it like a command," I said, knowing I'd regret it, but hating the disappointed look on his face too much to care. He gave me a confused look.

"Uh, Az, I really want to attend my lecture. Please do something so I can?" he said, his voice going up at the end as if he was asking a question.

Taking it as a command, I waved my hand at the bare wall across the room, and an image of his classroom appeared on it, the voices filling the room as if we were sitting in the classroom itself.

"What the... " Elijah mumbled as he stared at the wall. Then he turned to me, gratitude in his eyes as he popped up and pressed a kiss to my cheek, startling me. "Thank you so much!"

He turned back to the lecture, but I continued watching him. He was such a strange human. Lonely, with secrets he still hadn't shared with me. He'd summoned me without any ulterior motives. And his kiss had made my stomach react in ways I'd never experienced before. What was he and why did he make me feel this way? Like protecting him was my number-one goal in life, when every other time I'd been summoned, I'd secretly been counting down the days until I would be free?

08 | AZAZEL

My little human was driving me crazy.

I still hadn't figured out what it was he was hiding from me, the reason those kids had attacked him a few weeks ago. They'd kept their distance after that, and my glares had sent them packing whenever they got too close.

Elijah had waved off or just completely ignored my questions anytime I went near the topic, and I was getting tired of the evasion. Since he was the one who'd summoned me, I couldn't use my magic to make him talk either, though I was close to trying anyway.

"What are you thinking so seriously about?" the man in question asked, and I glanced up from my spot on the floor to where he sat on the couch, looking at something on his phone.

"Food," I answered, not wanting him to know how much space he took up in my thoughts.

Elijah flashed me a grin, chuckling as he pushed his glasses up his nose. They were always sliding off, as if they had a mind of their own. I hadn't told him I could make them stay if he wanted to because I enjoyed watching him, though I didn't want to look too closely at why *that* was. "Of course you are. Why am I not surprised? Do you wanna order something?"

Ordering something meant *do you want to look at these menus and then magic up some food for us?* It was what I'd been doing since I got here, and I'd apparently saved Elijah quite a bit of money.

"Nah, not yet. Let me think about it a bit more so I'm *really* hungry," I said, and his smile turned into a full-out belly-laugh.

"Damn, you're adorable," he said, and I raised my brows, staring at him like he was crazy. Which he obviously was if he actually meant that.

"I'm not adorable! I'm a demon. I'm fierce and dangerous, *monstrous* even."

"Oh, please. You're so far from a monster."

I waved at my face as if it explained everything, which it should. I had glowing red eyes and a definitely not-human face. Just to emphasize my point, I let my fangs peek out as I scowled at him.

"Is that supposed to scare me? You have a pretty face, Az," Elijah said with a shake of his head, and my eyes widened at this observation as realization struck and I sat up, staring at Elijah.

"Huh. Maybe that's it."

"What? What's it?"

"Maybe you have a few screws loose. That would explain things."

Elijah rolled his eyes and leaned forward until his face was at the same level, his eyes boring into mine.

As I returned his stare, his eyes roamed over me, and I felt an emotion I actively did everything in my power to bury deep within myself since it was a weakness. I felt self-conscious, and

I had a sudden urge to hide my face, which annoyed me and made me press my lips into a thin line, which I'm sure did nothing to improve my looks. What was this human doing to me?

"You might not be human, Az, but you definitely aren't ugly," he said finally, and I huffed, the weird feeling in my chest only getting stronger.

"Why are you doing that?"

"Doing what?" he asked with a puzzled frown.

"Handling me like a human. I'm a demon, Elijah. Have you forgotten that?"

He rolled his eyes. "So? You're still a person, Az. Just because you're a demon doesn't mean I should treat you any differently."

I screwed up my face, glaring at him. How had this conversation turned on me? Hadn't I been thinking about a way to find answers about his past?

I shook my head, shaking off his words and the thoughts in my head. Elijah placed a warm, soft palm on my cheek, stilling me. I blinked at him, exhaling a shaky breath. What was he doing to me?

"Elijah," I whispered, and then his tender lips were on mine, and everything disappeared. I gasped at the softness, and then moaned when his tongue slipped into my mouth. I'd taken great care to hide this particular trait of mine, but now there was no hiding the forked end of my tongue. I waited for him to jerk back, to pull away, but instead the tip of his tickled the spot where my tongue split, making me shiver.

I wasn't a very sexual demon on a good day, another fact that had separated me from the others in my realm. I usually needed a connection with my partner before I could be intimate with them in any capacity—and even then it was a bit of a hit and miss—and that wasn't something that happened easily in the demon realm. And yet kissing Elijah was the best experience of my life. When had this little human started to mean so much to me?

Elijah pulled away with a gasp, and I watched him, wondering how he'd react now. Would he tell me to forget it? Tell me he just wanted to see what it felt like to kiss a demon? It wouldn't be the first time someone said that to me, after all.

There had been a witch once, a long time ago, who'd summoned me to be her sex slave. I hadn't had a choice then, since a summoned demon had to follow their summoner's commands. I didn't like to think about that time much, but I'd learned enough to know that humans would always think of demons as someone lesser.

But Elijah didn't. Did he? I thought back to everything that'd happened since I was summoned by him, and I couldn't remember a single instance.

I blinked at him, waiting for him to say something. His eyes roamed over my face, as if he was trying to read me.

"Um," I said, and a grin spread across his face.

"Ha! Have I finally made the great demon Azazel speechless?"

I rolled my eyes at him, glad I couldn't blush. I imagined my cheeks would be bright red if I could, and that would be humiliating.

"Okay, how about we go out for dinner instead?" Elijah asked, blowing completely past the kiss and leaving me to wonder if he was planning to ignore it ever happened.

I blinked, not liking the fact that he kept surprising me. I didn't like it at all. I swear.

"Out?"

"Yep. If you want to, that is," he said, his cheeks coloring with the blush I'd been talking about. But while on other humans it looked stupid, it just made Elijah look prettier.

I found myself nodding, and the way his smile widened stopped me from telling him no like I should've. It wasn't like he'd commanded me to come with him, but I didn't want to disappoint him, and that was the *only* reason I'd said yes. Obviously, it wasn't because his question had sounded a hell of a lot like he was asking me out on a date. Not at all.

"I know this really great Thai restaurant we can go to," he said, and I realized his palm was still pressed against my cheek.

"Sounds good," I agreed, carefully leaning into his touch. The great demon Azazel going on a date with a human. Who would've thought?

09 | ELIJAH

WHEN I SUMMONED A demon, I probably wasn't supposed to kiss said demon. I definitely wasn't supposed to take him out on a date.

Then again, when had I ever done what I was supposed to?

Even after everything that had gone down last year, I'd refused to move to a new state like I was supposed to. I'd had nothing to do with what my father had done, and I'd refused to run away like I'd been party to his crimes. And that might make me a stubborn idiot who was hated by practically everyone in town, but I didn't care. I liked living here, and I wasn't going to let people run me off for something I hadn't done.

"Elijah, what are we doing?" Azazel asked, honestly sounding a bit puzzled.

"Having dinner, of course," I answered with raised brows. I wanted to tease him just a little, since it was usually he who had the upper hand in our conversations.

"I know that. I mean, are you...is this...a date?"

I'd never heard him sound quite like that. It was a mixture of confusion and...nerves? I decided to go easy on him and answer his question.

"Yep, it's a date, Azazel. If you want it to be, of course. Or it can just be two friends having dinner," I added with a shrug, though I hoped he wanted it to be a date as well. I didn't know when it'd happened, but I liked Az. I'd found him attractive since the moment I saw him—I didn't think many allosexual gay men would've been able to resist him with that huge-ass dick of his on full display—but the more time I'd spent with him, the more I'd liked him for who he was.

He watched me for a long moment and then leaned forward, his voice lowering as he said, "If you want to bed me, you could just tell me to do whatever you want, you know? You don't have to do all of this," he said, waving at the restaurant around us. It wasn't anything fancy, but it was a nice place, with low lighting and intimate tables, soft music in the background.

Any other time, I would've teased him for using the phrase *bed me*. But all I could think about was what he was saying, and the implication it contained. Had someone who'd summoned him done that to him before? Told him to have sex with them, without his consent?

And was that why he'd kissed me back? Because I—his summoner—had initiated it, and not because he wanted it? I felt a chill spread through my insides, and I had to swallow hard before I could speak.

I narrowed my eyes as I leaned forward, so close our noses almost touched. "Listen to me, Az. I will never, *ever* tell you to do something you don't want to. If you don't want to have dinner with me right now, I won't stop you from leaving. Anything we do will be because both of us want it. And I'm really, really sorry I didn't ask before I kissed you. I didn't realize you wouldn't have a choice about kissing me back. If...if you hadn't wanted that, if you don't want *this*, we can leave."

Azazel blinked at me, then again. And again. Had I broken him?

"Azazel?"

Finally, after what felt like hours, he nodded and sat back, his fingers drumming the table for a moment before he picked up the menu and glanced at me over it. "So, what are we having?"

I smiled as relief washed over me and sat back in my seat, picking up my own menu and answering his question.

As we talked over a delicious dinner, I couldn't help wondering about Azazel's past. I hadn't really given it much thought, but now that I was thinking about it, I couldn't stop. Had he been summoned to the human realm a lot? What were his previous summoners like? Had they misused their power over him?

I also realized I should've thought about this before I initiated anything with him. No matter how much I liked him, he was still practically enslaved to me. He had to follow all my orders. The power imbalance couldn't be removed from the equation, and it wasn't right for me to pursue Az.

"Elijah?" I blinked up at Az, surprised to realize I'd cleared my plate, and so had he. How long had I been lost in thought?

"Yeah?"

"Thank you for taking me out on this date. I really enjoyed it," he said, sounding like he truly meant it. I smiled widely as I realized what he was indirectly saying in his very special way. He'd confirmed that he wanted this to be considered a date. My feelings weren't one-sided, and maybe, maybe pursuing this wouldn't be a complete disaster.

"Only the best for my precious demon," I said, only half-joking, and Az blinked again, his brown I'm-trying-to-look-like-a-human eyes flashing red for a second, as if he couldn't quite control his emotions, and I felt a weird spark of pleasure at having affected him.

"Come on, it's time for an after-dinner walk. We'll get ice cream for dessert," I said, and his eyes lit up at the thought. He was so easy to please.

After I'd paid for our food—since I'd asked him out, I declined his offer to use his magic to pay our bill because it didn't feel right—I led Az out of the restaurant, and we started walking. He startled when I took his hand in mine, his eyes shooting to mine. In this form, we were the same height, so I merely leaned over and kissed the tip of his nose, winking as I pulled back.

His eyes flashed red again, and I smiled to myself.

A part of me wanted to tell him everything about my past, everything that had made me a pariah in the town I'd grown up in. Everything he'd been so curious about. But tonight felt too... right, too good, to muddle it with talk of the past. I didn't want my past to intrude on this moment and sully it.

I'll tell him some other time, I decided to myself, squeezing Az's hand. Tonight was for Azazel and me.

"Ice cream!" Az exclaimed a few minutes later, and I laughed as he practically dragged me to an ice cream van of all things. "I can't pick," he pouted, his eyes taking in all the different flavors.

"Can we please get one scoop of each?" I asked, knowing full well there were at least twelve flavors in there.

The ice cream guy raised a brow at me as he lifted his scoop. "One of each? You sure?"

I glanced over at Az, whose eyes were practically sparkling as he looked at me, and smiled. "Yep, I'm sure. Give us four at first, please."

Then, we demolished twelve scoops. Well, I merely took a bite of each flavor, while Az ate the rest, looking for all the world like I'd given him the moon.

Once I'd paid up, we walked toward home hand in hand, Azazel's a little sticky with ice cream residue.

It was the best date of my life.

10 | Azazel

I HADN'T TOLD ELIJAH this, but tonight was the first date I'd ever been on. I didn't remember my human life. It'd been too long ago, and once I became a demon, there weren't many people interested in anything more than a simple fuck. No one had ever bought me dinner and all the ice cream I wanted, and I didn't quite know what to do with the weird fluttery feeling in my gut.

Elijah was human. He'd summoned me. He could make me do anything. And yet he'd told me, firmly and with ill-concealed anger, that he would never make me do anything I didn't want to.

I'd been summoned many times since Underworld was closed down, since demons stopped being the deliverers of torture, and none of my summoners had ever cared about what I wanted. Was it because all my previous summoners had been magic users? Was it Elijah's humanity that made him different? Or was it just him?

"You look like you're thinking some deep thoughts." I looked up at Elijah, who lay on the edge of his bed, looking down at me. I hadn't wanted to go back to the demon realm tonight, so I'd decided to bunker down beside his bed, though I'd replaced the sleeping bag he'd offered me my first day here with a thick quilt after he told me to *get comfortable.*

"Food. I'm thinking about food," I deadpanned, and he rolled his eyes.

"If you're thinking about food after eating all that ice cream, then you must have a black hole in that stomach of yours," he said, and I grinned. I raised my hand up and poked his nose, jerking away when he batted at my hand.

"You know... I've never dated anyone before," I said, hoping he wouldn't make a big deal out of it, but knowing he probably would. He was a bit of a drama queen sometimes.

As predicted, his eyes widened behind his glasses, and he leaned forward, his copper curls falling into his face as he almost toppled off the bed. "Really? Never?"

I shrugged. "Demons usually like to just jump straight into bed, and that's not my thing. And people of this realm, well, I do what they tell me to, and no one has ever told me to go on a date with them."

"Their loss," Elijah said, his lips pressing into a firm line. "You're annoying sometimes, but you're also really sweet, Az. And for the record, I've never dated anyone either."

"I find that hard to believe. You must have guys clamoring." How couldn't he? He was gorgeous, sassy, and a little nerdy but in a cute way. If that wasn't the perfect mix, I didn't know what was.

"Uh-huh. Like you haven't seen how popular I am around here."

This was the first time Elijah had brought up the fact, and I had to admit I wanted to pry. I wanted to know why the kids in his school avoided him, what that asshole had meant, if Elijah's parents had something to do with the whole thing, but I wasn't sure if he'd tell me.

"Come on, ask me. I know you want to," he said when I hadn't said anything for a few minutes.

I gazed up at him, at the wry look on his face. "What happened, Elijah?"

He blew out a deep breath, making his curls bob, and I couldn't help wrapping a curl around my finger. The copper contrasted beautifully with my dark skin, and Elijah turned his gaze to my hand as he spoke. "A year ago, the cops arrested my father. At first, they said it was just to ask him some questions, but then it turned out that he... that he'd been murdering kids. Boys of different ages. They didn't tell us all the details, but he... he raped them, tortured them, and then killed them. Eight boys, Az. He killed eight boys before he was caught."

I'd known something had happened in his past, but I'd never expected it to be something so gruesome. Before I could figure out what to say, he continued, "And you know the scariest part? My father was the only parent I had. My mom left us when I was around three, and I used to think my father was the best dad in the world."

"Some people are good at living double lives," I said. "He could be the best dad without being a good human being." It wasn't like I hadn't come across similar people when I used to torture the black souls of Underworld, back before Underworld was declared obsolete and shut down.

"You know, I'd believe that, Az, if I hadn't seen the boys' pictures. Copper curls, hazel eyes, tall for their ages. Sound familiar?" Elijah said it without inflection, as if he couldn't care less, but I could hear the pain and fear he was trying to hide.

It wasn't hard to understand what he was implying, and my blood boiled at the thought of his father hurting him that way. Had he killed those kids to curb his temptation for his own son? Or had he always planned to make Elijah one of his victims?

"Where's your father now?" I asked, mentally planning a visit to give him a taste of his own medicine.

"Hell, probably. Apparently, criminals have low tolerance for pedophile murderers. He was killed a month after he was sent to prison."

"Then the Burning Chasm will take care of him," I said, wishing for the first time that I was still the torturer of Underworld I used to be centuries ago. I'd hated my job, but I was suddenly feeling very torture-y.

"That's the place where the evil souls are always burning, right? You think my father ended up there?"

"Trust me. There's no redeeming that kind of man. He'll suffer for what he did to those boys, for what he did to you."

Elijah blew out a sigh, his face drawn as memories of the past haunted him. In an attempt to pull him back to the present, I leaned up on my arms and pressed my lips to his in a light, barely there kiss.

Before I could pull away, his hand wrapped around the stub of my horn, and he pressed closer, kissing me deeply as his tongue snuck into my mouth. I moaned when he teased the space between the fork in my tongue, and he hummed softly.

His cheeks were flushed when he pulled away, and he watched me, his eyes dark. He gave me a cautious look as he asked, "Can you sleep up here instead?" He looked like he expected me to say no, but he also looked like he needed someone to hold him together.

When the fuck had I grown so mushy?

And yet, despite my hatred for all things soft, I found myself nodding. His bed was too small for me, so I used a bit of my magic to enlarge it to fit me. Elijah cuddled into my side, pressing his face into my chest. He was asleep within minutes, but I lay there for much longer, wondering how it'd come to this.

How had I ended up falling for this bright-eyed, curly-haired human?

11 | ELIJAH

Sooooo... I might have been falling for a demon. No big deal, right? I mean, he wasn't *evil*. Honestly, he was a sweetheart most of the times, though he could be an ass sometimes. He was like a coconut, grumpy on the outside and a total softie on the inside. The way he'd held me last night—and every other night I'd asked since that first time after our first date—was proof of that.

It *was* quick, though, the way I felt for him. I hadn't known him that long, after all. It had barely been three months since I'd summoned him. How could I be sure my feelings were real and not just my loneliness making me feel something that wasn't there? And what about Az? Did he feel the same about me? Could he? Or did he just think of me as the *little human* he had to entertain for a year?

And what if he was only doing this because he thought it was part of his 'duties?' Had I taken advantage of our power imbalance by asking him out? After all, it wasn't like he could say no to me, right?

Oh my God, had I been forcing him all along? I felt nauseous at the thought, and I squeezed my eyes shut.

I knew he'd enjoyed the dates, but that didn't mean he had feelings for me, right? That didn't mean he had wanted to actually go out with me. Oh my God, how could I have been so stupid?

An oomph escaped me as a large, obsidian arm fell over me, pinning me to the bed. Az lay on his stomach beside me, his soft snores the only sound in the room.

Was I overreacting? After our first date, Az had told me he enjoyed it, and he'd said that after practically every date. He kissed me back, and sometimes he even initiated. Surely he wouldn't do that if he didn't actually feel anything for me, right?

I glanced over at the clock and realized I'd be late if I didn't get up now. Okay, crisis later, classes now. I tried to heave Az's arm off me, but he didn't so much as budge.

"Az, lemme go. I need to get ready for school!" I groaned, pushing at him with zero results.

Narrowing my eyes, I turned my head and blew air right into his ear. He jerked awake instantly, his red eyes flashing as he looked around the room.

"Hi, hello. Can you stop pinning me down, please? I'm going to be late for school!"

He blinked at me for a couple of moments before rolling over to the other side. I hurried to my feet, cursing under my breath as I realized I didn't even have enough time for a shower.

I froze as I felt Az's magic surround me—I wasn't quite sure how I could recognize his magic when I couldn't see it, but I just knew that's what the warmth around me was—and when it disappeared, I felt refreshed, and my clothes had changed.

"Did you just give me a magical dry shower?" I asked, finding Az in his human form and looking ready even though less than a minute earlier he'd been snoring his ass off.

"I think the phrase you're looking for is thank you," he sassed back, and I rolled my eyes as I grabbed my bag.

"Come on, then. The first lecture will be starting soon."

"Yay," Az deadpanned, and I couldn't help but chuckle as I led the way out. He hated my classes more than anything in the world, and yet he sat through them all even though I'd never asked him to. Surely, that meant he felt something for me. Why else would he do that?

We made it to the lecture with seconds to spare, and everything was like every other day. The assholes from before kept their distance, like they knew better than to cross Az again.

Things changed when we were in the small campus cafeteria. Specifically, when Az kissed my cheek before taking the seat next to me. He'd never done that before, not once in the month since we'd started dating. A hush fell over the students, and I could almost feel the eyes on me.

I ignored them the best I could, hunching down in my seat as much as a six-foot-tall guy could and focusing on my meal, but I couldn't quite block out all the whispers.

"Did that guy just kiss him?"

"He's new. Maybe he doesn't know."

"Or maybe he's some kind of freak who is into that kind of shit."

A loud bang startled the shit out of me, and I whipped my head around to see the table behind us had fallen on its side, all the legs on one side broken in half. It was the same table the whispers had been coming from, and now the people there had laps full of food as they sat still, too stunned to move.

I bit my lip to keep from laughing as I glared at Az, or at least tried to. I was too amused to really give a fuck, and the twinkle in his eyes told me Az knew.

"What a weird accident, huh?" he said, humor lacing each word.

"Indeed," I agreed as I stuffed my mouth full of the gooey pasta.

I'd spent way too long keeping my head down, listening as all these people hated me for something I'd had no part in. I was a victim of my father's deeds too, but somehow, no one could see that. They had no idea what it felt like to know the person you'd looked up to your whole life was a monster, a monster who'd hurt kids in your name, who'd probably been planning to hurt *you* someday. No one understood how I felt, no one except Azazel.

It didn't matter what they thought, though. I didn't need friends who would bail at the first sign of trouble. I had a demon who would do anything for me, and he was all I needed.

Now all I needed to do was figure out if he felt the same way about me, and if so, I needed to find a way to keep him with me after our year-long contract ended. It'd only been three months, and already I wanted Az to stay with me forever.

When we returned home, I worked on an assignment I needed to submit next week while Az played games on my phone. He was hooked on *Candy Crush* for some reason, and I left him to it as I worked, thinking about everything that had happened since I'd summoned him.

I'd never, ever expected it to work, but it had. I'd summoned Azazel, an eight-foot-tall obsidian demon with red eyes and broken horns who'd never been on a date and was intensely protective. Sometimes, I wondered if all of this was nothing but a giant hallucination, if I wasn't in some padded room after having a mental breakdown. After everything that went down with my father, it would make sense too, wouldn't it? But even in my wildest dreams, I couldn't have imagined someone as complicated and as perfect as Azazel.

He was sassy and an utter jerk in the beginning, but now that I knew him better, I could see it'd been his way of keeping me at a distance so I wouldn't be able to hurt him. Because someone in his past had. Maybe the same someone who'd treated him like a sex slave without his consent.

I wondered if he'd ever want to talk about that. I didn't want to pry, but I still wasn't sure if he understood just how much I'd meant it when I'd told him I'd never ask him to do something he didn't want to. I felt like it was a hard concept for him to get through his somewhat thick skull, but I hoped he'd realize it soon enough.

I glanced over to where he lay on the floor, feet up on the edge of the couch as he played, Hella—who'd come over for a visit but would probably disappear before bedtime—pressed against his side, her head resting on his hip as she napped. The tips of his tongue stuck out of his mouth as he clicked around the game, and I wanted to abandon my work to go kiss the hell out of him.

When he looked up at me with his red eyes glowing and raised a brow in invitation, I did just that. Hella did not like getting interrupted during her nap, and after she'd growled at me—she wasn't a fan of the puny human her demon owner liked spending time with, for some reason—she disappeared into thin air, leaving Az all to me.

12 | AZAZEL

Being a human's lover was... interesting. It was also weird and a little confusing. It'd been a month and a half since our first date, and since then, Elijah and I had gone out many times.

Things at his school had calmed down, and while some idiots still whispered about my human, I'd started blocking their voices with my magic so they wouldn't bother Elijah. My human was strong, but that didn't mean he had to suffer through their cruelty. Not if I could protect him from it. And since I was using my magic to make his life better, I didn't need his explicit permission, which was good because knowing him he'd tell me he deserved to hear it or some stupid shit like that.

But let's go back to my confusion. The reason our relationship had me so puzzled was the fact that Elijah hadn't tried to take it past kissing. From my in-depth study of humans on my off-time, I knew humans usually didn't wait so long to jump into bed with their lovers. At least not if they truly wanted them. Hell, some humans even jumped into bed without asking their partner's name if the attraction was strong enough.

Was that it then? Elijah liked me, but he wasn't attracted to my physical form?

I glanced down at myself and tried to see myself the way Elijah did. I was a foot and a half taller than him, large all over. I had a weird tongue—though Elijah did seem to enjoy playing with it when we kissed—and my eyes were scary. My skin color was very much unlike a human's, and so was my dick, not that he'd seen it yet. The only time he'd seen me naked was when I'd first shown up here, and the difference wouldn't have been visible then.

For fuck's sake, I was a demon. I wasn't supposed to act like this. I wasn't supposed to feel bloody *insecure,* especially not if a human didn't want to have sex with me. After all, wasn't that exactly what I'd hoped for when Elijah summoned me?

Then again, I'd never been a very good demon, had I? I'd done my job as well as any of the others, but other than that, I'd sucked. I never indulged in the orgies that even the Other-worlders had heard about—and were rumored to participate in. I didn't have fuck buddies for every day of the week, I wasn't kinky, and I hadn't even enjoyed the pain and torture I used to inflict on the dark souls way back when.

"What's on your mind?" Elijah asked as he plopped onto the couch beside me, his amber eyes bright behind his glasses, his copper curls as bouncy as ever. He was such a pretty human.

"Nothing," I answered quickly, but it was clear he didn't believe me. Hell, I wouldn't believe me.

Raising a brow, he sat up before straddling my thighs. My breath hitched as he settled in my lap, his palms on my shoulders as he gazed up into my eyes.

"Don't lie to me, Az. Tell me what's wrong. Please?" His thumbs caressed my collarbone, and I hummed deep in my chest at how good his touch felt. He wasn't trying to order me, and so the compulsion to answer him wasn't as strong as it would've been.

"I was worried... never mind." I shook my head. I was being an idiot. I didn't want to reveal this vulnerability to Elijah. I liked the way he saw me. To him, I was the big, powerful demon who could do anything, who could beat up his bullies and gently torture the people bad-mouthing him. Not the useless demon attacked by insecurities he'd never realized he had.

"Az, come on. How about this? If you tell me, I'll take the day off from school tomorrow, and we can go wherever you like."

"A week," I countered, because it was too tempting an offer to refuse, and I was nothing if not a great negotiator.

"Ha ha, no. How about two days?"

"Six."

"Three, and that's my final offer."

I sighed, knowing him well enough to know he wouldn't budge further. After all, that was why I'd started with an impossible number. "All right, deal. A long weekend."

"Only if you tell me," he reminded me, and I sighed.

"I was being an idiot," I grumbled, and as Elijah opened his mouth again, I waved him off. "Let me continue. I was just thinking that it's been more than a month since we started... dating, and you've... you haven't wanted to do anything more than kissing. And I thought maybe it was because of how I looked. I mean, I'm not exactly hu—"

"Stop talking." Elijah cut me off, and I snapped my mouth shut, my teeth clacking together with how harsh I was. He drew his palms up my neck until he was cupping my face, and then he shook his head.

"You crazy demon. How long have you been stewing over this? First off, I love the way you look, all right? You're bigger than me, which is a plus. Your tongue is literally magic. It's so fucking good. Your muscles are so yummy. I'd lick you all over if you let me. You're gorgeous, Az. Secondly, you have absolutely no freaking idea how much I've been holding back. The only reason I didn't ask to do all the things I want to do to you is because I want it to be your choice. You told me you don't like casual sex, and you've implied more than once that one of your previous summoners didn't exactly care about your consent. Whatever we do, I want it to be your choice. And that's the only reason I haven't devoured you, okay?"

Elijah exhaled loudly as he finished his rant, his palms holding my face tighter than necessary. His grip loosened as he realized that, and he dragged his right palm up until his fingers were in my hair, the tips tickling the edge of my broken horn and making me shiver.

"I didn't realize," I murmured, too stunned to say anything else. Elijah had been insistent about never asking me to do anything I wouldn't want to do, but I hadn't realized it would be the same for things like this. I'd done a lot of things—sexually speaking—and if I was honest with myself, which I usually wasn't in this case, I hadn't wanted to do most of it. But I'd done it because I'd been told to.

But now here was this human who was giving me something I hadn't had in a very long time: a choice, free will.

And it wasn't difficult at all to choose to lean forward and press my lips to his, to show him exactly what I wanted.

"I still need your words, Azazel," he mumbled against my lips, and I smiled even as frustration coursed through me.

"I want you to kiss me, my little human. And I want to suck you until you come. I want to sink into you and make you come over and over again. I want it all with you. Is that enough words for you?" I sassed, licking his lower lip with the tips of my tongue. Everything I'd said was true. I did want it now, but I wondered distantly if I'd just given him a blanket approval for the future. I knew Elijah enough to know he'd ask me every time, and something in my chest relaxed at that thought.

Elijah groaned and attacked my mouth in a flurry of lips and tongue and teeth, and I pulled him to me, soaking up every ounce of touch and affection like I was starved for it. And maybe I was because I never, ever wanted to stop.

13 | ELIJAH

"So, what do you want to do?" I asked as I pulled back, my breathing harsh. Azazel was a phenomenal kisser, and I was addicted to his tongue. It was slimmer than a human's, and the way he reacted when I brushed the spot where it split into two was just magnificent.

As I watched, he swiped that same lethal tongue over his bottom lip, his eyes roaming over me, his gaze so intense I could almost feel it caressing me. I shivered as his eyes met mine again, and he smirked in his trademark way.

"I want to taste you."

My breath caught at the image of his wicked tongue playing with my cock, and I bit back a moan. "I...I'd like that."

He grinned, and I gasped as he picked me off his lap, lifting until my legs were thrown over his shoulders. Cradling my ass, he looked up at me, his eyes so dark that only a ring of red shone through. "I'm going to blow you just like this. Don't worry. I won't let you fall."

I grabbed the backrest despite his reassurance, and I was glad I did because a moment later I almost fell forward when cool air hit my ass, and I realized Az had used his magic to remove my pants and underwear.

"Fuck, you look delicious," Az murmured, and I felt myself blushing. I didn't do shit like this. I'd hooked up before, but I'd never been with someone I had actual feelings for. And even when I'd hooked up, it'd never been...adventurous. A blowjob in a club bathroom, a hard fuck and then goodbye. No one had ever manhandled me. Not like Az was doing it, as if I wasn't a lanky, six-foot dude, as if I was weightless.

I shivered as he traced a line up my inner thigh with the tip of his nose, whimpering when his tongue snaked out, lightning quick, to lick my balls with the lightest of touches.

Az hummed softly, completely focused on what he was doing. Trusting him to not let me fall, I placed one palm on his scalp, tracing the edge of his broken horn with the tip of my finger because I knew it drove him crazy. He still hadn't told me the story of how they'd ended up that way except for what he'd said about not being demonic enough, but I knew he would when he was ready.

"Holy shit!" I gasped as he swallowed my cock, taking it all into his mouth in one go. I had not been expecting that. My size was in proportion to the rest of me, and while I didn't have a lot of girth, I was long enough that it took most guys a while to work up to it. But Az wasn't just any guy. He was a demon with a wicked tongue, now wreaking havoc to the tip of my cock.

My back arched as the tips of his tongue entered my slit, and only Azazel's grip on my ass kept me from falling. I didn't have enough brain power to worry because all my blood had rushed south.

"Fuck, Az, that feels so good," I said, my voice breaking halfway as his throat closed around my length. He swallowed again and again, using his throat to drive me crazy. Clearly, he hadn't even heard of a gag reflex.

He hummed around my length and squeezed my ass, using his grip to push me even deeper into his mouth. I groaned loudly, too lost for words. I placed both hands on his head, scraping my nails through his short hair, and rubbed the base of his horns, loving the way it made him hum around my cock.

Using his grip on my ass, he started thrusting my cock into his mouth, controlling the movement completely as he used me to fuck his mouth. It was already the best blowjob I'd ever had, and I hadn't even come yet.

"Fuck, Az. I'm close," I gasped, feeling the familiar tingle down my spine, though I knew this climax would be unlike any I'd ever experienced before.

He squeezed my ass tighter in answer and quickened his pace, his nose rubbing into my groin with each thrust. The tips of his tongue slipped inside my slit once again, and I was gone.

My back arched, and I might have screamed his name, but I couldn't be sure. The only thing I was sure of was that nothing had ever felt as good as this. Az swallowed my cum, his tongue lapping at my cock to get every drop of it.

I went boneless in his grip, and he still didn't let me fall as he slowly slid me back into his lap. And onto his very hard erection that pressed against my ass through his pants.

I pressed my palm to it, rubbing it slowly, and Azazel gave a full-body shudder, pushing into my touch before he took my hand in his, pulling it away from his cock.

"What...won't you let me make you feel good?" I asked, and Az smiled hesitantly.

"You did. What we just did? It was the best thing I've ever experienced. I don't need anything else. I promise."

I stared at him, trying to gauge if he was telling the truth. While he looked like he meant it, I also felt like he wasn't telling me everything.

Squinting at him, I placed my palm on his cheek and met his eyes. "You know that no matter what we do here, it doesn't mean you owe me anything, right? I'll respect your wishes if you never want to do this again, or if you only want to do it sometimes. If you say yes, I won't take it as carte blanche to do anything I want, you know. You can still always say no."

Az watched me for a moment, and I wondered if maybe he had just been saying no and now I'd made things weird. But then he took my palm from his cheek and placed it over his erection.

Smiling, I rose up on my knees and pressed my lips to his, kissing him softly and humming when I realized I could taste myself. Then, I sat back, rubbing his erection through his pants as I stared at him.

"You, Azazel, are the sweetest, most talented person I've ever met. I'm so lucky I found that book and that I was crazy enough to actually try summoning you."

Azazel chuckled, the tips of his tongue sneaking out to lick his lips. "Trust me. No one is happier about that than me. You're a good human."

Warmth fluttered in my chest, and I shifted back before tugging at his pants pointedly. With an amused huff, he made them disappear, and I got my first look at his hard cock.

I whistled softly, taking in the decidedly inhuman cock in front of me. When he'd first arrived, he hadn't been hard, and I'd consciously avoided looking at his groin. Which was why I hadn't known that his cock had ridges on it, slim bumps that ran the length.

Reaching out, I brushed my finger over one of the ridges, and Azazel shuddered under me. He'd been holding himself stiff as he waited for my reaction, and I could imagine what he was thinking after the things he'd said earlier.

To make sure he had no doubts about how I felt, I got off his lap and went down on my knees, spreading his legs open and crawling into the space between them. He sat forward to help me along, and I grinned up at him before turning my focus onto his cock.

Wrapping my palm around him, I ran it over his cock from base to head, humming at how good it felt. I wondered how it would feel inside me; the ridges would feel amazing rubbing against my hole.

Leaning forward, I ran my tongue over his tip, tasting his salty-sweet precum. I was nowhere near as good as him at giving blowjobs, but I did my best, laving my tongue over his cock before wrapping my lips around the head.

It didn't take long to make Az come, and when he did, he went completely still before his cum filled my mouth, and I swallowed as much as I could. Apparently, demons came a lot more than us puny humans, and I had to let some of it drip down my chin to avoid choking.

"Wow," Azazel said, his voice all but inaudible. Chuckling, I sat up and fell onto the couch beside him. He casually waved a hand, and the cum trailing down my chin disappeared, and our pants reappeared.

Let out a weary laugh, I crawled over to him and fell sideways into his lap. He wrapped his arms around me like I'd wanted him to, and I snuggled into him, letting the comfort of his hold wash over me as the sleepy haze of a good orgasm—and the enjoyment of getting to give the same to Az—washed over me.

Whether it was fate that led me to find that book that day, or just dumb luck, I was grateful for the man it'd led me to, and I'd do anything to hold on to him.

14 | Azazel

It'd been six months since Elijah summoned me, and I'd never been happier. Every day with my little human was better than the last, and I'd stopped waiting for the other shoe to drop, finally trusting the fact that Elijah truly was as good as he'd first seemed.

The other humans at his place of learning had learned to not bother him, and while he never complained, I worried about him. Didn't humans need frequent socialization and people who cared about them?

Granted, I cared about him a lot, but was I enough? Didn't he need someone who could relate to him better?

If he asked, I could bring him a human who would happily befriend him, but I didn't think he'd approve.

Which was why I was in the demon realm while Elijah attended his boring classes, hoping to get advice from my one real friend besides Hella.

"Azzy boy! So you didn't fall into the Chasm after all," my friend-slash-pain-in-the-ass said as she slithered over from wherever she'd been hiding.

She was a gorgeous demon, with deep red hair that fell to her waist, bright yellow eyes, and a curvy frame that gave the best hugs on the rare occasion she felt like one. The lower half of her body was that of a snake, with deep red scales that gleamed whenever the light fell on them.

We weren't quite sure why demons had such different body types, but the oldest of us said it had something to do with the magic we'd possessed in our human lives. I had no memories of that time, so I couldn't say if he was right, though it seemed as fitting a theory as any.

"Fressia." I greeted her with a tilt of my head, and she flashed me a fanged grin.

"Tell me," she demanded, raising a single brow at me.

"Tell you what?"

"About whatever put that look on your face. Let me guess. It's the human, isn't it? Your summoner."

I shook my head, amazed as always at how well she could read me. "His name is Elijah," I found myself saying, even though I made it a habit of calling him my little human. But that was the thing, wasn't it? He was *my* human. Not Fressia's or anyone else's.

"Elijah," she said in a lilting voice, her eyes almost sparkling with mischief.

"Stop it. Or I'm leaving," I threatened, and she sighed as if *I* was the one being a pain in the ass.

"Fine, fine. So what do you need help with? Are you going to tell me or do I have to start guessing?"

Knowing the kind of things she'd guess, I waved her off. "I'll talk." I sighed softly before explaining Elijah's friendlessness to her.

"Is that all?" she asked, and I glared at her. I didn't like her implication that it wasn't a big deal. I was worried about Elijah. I didn't want him to be left alone once our year together was up.

"I just mean there's an easy solution to this," she clarified, staying me with a raised palm as if I was about to attack. Even if I'd wanted to, I knew better than to take a risk like that. Fressia was lethal.

"You think so? What can I do?" I asked, not worried about sounding too eager at the moment. Showing emotion wasn't something demons were used to, but I found it easier the longer I lived with Elijah.

"Bring him here," she said, and I shook my head, sure I'd heard her wrong. "You said he doesn't get along with humans, so maybe he'd get along with us."

"I'm sorry. Did I hear you right? You want me to bring Elijah, a human, into the demon realm? Have you lost your damn mind?"

Fressia's eyes narrowed, and I immediately regretted my words, no matter how true they were. Still, I forged on. "Even if I wanted to, which I don't, it would be impossible. Only the dead are allowed, remember?"

Fressia waved it off as if my words meant nothing. "There are always loopholes, sweetheart. Remember how King Damien brought his human mates to Otherworld? They're both still very much living. In fact, from what I hear, their bond returned some of King Damien's humanity."

Of course I'd heard about King Damien and his unique mating. Everyone in the demon realm had. But there was one major difference between the king and my situation. "They were his mates, Fressia. Elijah is just my summoner. Nothing more."

The lie tasted bitter on my tongue. No matter how much I'd wanted Elijah to just be my summoner, he was so much more now. He'd wiggled his way into my demon heart with his sass and his sweetness, and I didn't know what would happen once our time together ended. To be quite honest, I didn't like thinking about our time together ending.

"I know that. What I meant was with magic, there are always loopholes. You can't bring a human into the demon realm, sure. But what happens if your summoner orders you to take him to the demon realm? Which is more powerful? The magic that compels us to do our summoner's bidding or the one that keeps the living out of the demon realm?"

I blinked at her, not having an answer for her question. No summoner had ever asked to visit the demon realm, as far as I knew, but I could very well imagine Elijah doing just that.

The question was—could the magic of the realms be tricked into letting a human into a realm no living human had ever seen? And if it could, did I want that? Did I want to bring the brightness that was Elijah into my dark realm?

Would seeing my home make him finally realize what I truly was? Would it change the way he felt about me? And would I let that risk stop me from doing something that could potentially be beneficial to him?

15 | ELIJAH

Azazel was acting weird. It wasn't unusual for him to act...let's say quirky...but this felt like something different.

Ever since we'd started dating, he'd been more open with me, even about stuff he felt was stupid or he was insecure about. Yet, for the past few days, I'd been catching him watching me when he thought I wasn't looking, and I really wanted to know what was going on in his head.

I'd tried asking him point blank, but he just denied anything even being wrong. It'd been the same every time I asked, and it had all started the day he'd last gone to the demon realm.

Something must have happened there, but what? Had someone said something? Was he required to return and was trying to figure out a way to break the news to me?

I'd always known we had an expiration date, but to me it was still six months away. I didn't know how to deal with the thought that I only had a few more days left with Az.

Served me right for falling in love with a demon.

I blinked, startled at the thought. Was I really in love with the annoying demon I'd summoned six months ago? How did this happen?

It didn't matter how, did it? The fact was I was in love with the stupid demon who was keeping stupid secrets from me, probably trying to figure out a way to tell me we were over.

What if I was the only one who'd been idiotic enough to involve feelings? It felt like it meant something whenever Azazel kissed me, but was that just wishful thinking?

What if I was a ticket to the human realm and a good time to Az? Did I dare ask? Should I let things continue as they were and wait for him to say something?

I rolled my eyes at myself. Yeah, right. Like I'd ever just stay quiet and ignore the problem. I was more the kind to face the problem head-on and then deal with the consequences later. Fuck waiting and fuck Az for making me doubt everything.

He'd bowed out of coming to classes with me again, so the moment I got home today, I'd demand he tell me everything, no matter how bad it was.

Decision made, I focused back on the lecture I'd been ignoring, my mind clearer than it'd been all week now that I had a plan.

When I got home, Az was waiting for me like always, a feast ready on the coffee table that I had a hard time ignoring. But no, I had to focus. I needed answers.

Carefully, I removed my shoes, placed my bag in its nook, and settled on the couch. Then, throwing out the carefully planned speech I'd worked on while walking home, I blurted out, "Are you leaving?"

Az's eyes widened, the red flashing brighter, and he asked, "Do you...want me to?"

I rolled my eyes. "Of course not," I grumbled, pushing my curls off my forehead. "But it feels like you are. Like you're trying to figure out how to tell me or something. You've been acting weird ever since your last visit home, and I thought maybe you need to go back for good or something."

Without uttering a word, Az sat down beside me and wrapped his arms around me, pulling me into a tight hug. Have you ever cozied up in one of those weighted blankets that feel like warmth and comfort and safety all rolled into one? That's what Az's hugs felt like, and I immediately relaxed into him.

"I'm not going anywhere, my little human. I promise."

"Then what—"

"I'm getting there," he interrupted me with a soft chuckle, and I huffed as I snuggled deeper into him. "When I was visiting, a friend made a suggestion I haven't been able to stop thinking about."

"Oh?"

He hummed, his chest vibrating against my cheek. This was much, much better than a weighted blanket.

"She suggested I bring you to the demon realm," he admitted, and I jerked upright, my eyes widening.

I pushed up my askew glasses as I looked into his eyes. "You can do that? Take me to see your home?"

"Living humans aren't allowed in the realm. Hell, now that we no longer punish souls, *no* humans are allowed there."

"Then how..." I trailed off, but he knew what I was asking.

"Fressia, my friend, had a theory that if you ordered me to take you, it might work, since demons are required to fulfill their summoner's every request."

"Has anyone ever done that before?" I asked, though my mind was already thinking about visiting the demon realm and what it'd be like. But then I remembered Az hadn't told me about this until I'd demanded answers, and I wondered if maybe he didn't want me coming to his home world. Why else would he have hesitated?

"Not that I know of. It was why I hadn't mentioned it. I didn't want you to be disappointed."

While he sounded sincere, I had a feeling there was more to it. The challenge would be trying to figure out what.

"Why don't you want me to visit the demon realm?" Guess we were cutting straight to the chase then.

Az sighed and looked away, though his arms stayed wrapped around me. He might've even tightened his hold as he spoke. "It's not that I don't want you to visit. It's just...it's not a happy place. And you, well, you're the brightest thing in my life. I guess I don't want you to realize how dark my world is, how dark *I* am."

I stared at him, gobsmacked. Was he for real right now?

"You magicked me a ball pit last weekend. And then you spent the whole afternoon playing in it with me. Trust me. I already know how *dark* you are, you big goof. Nothing will change the way I feel about you. Don't you know that already?"

I rose up on my knees and kissed him before he could reply. I didn't want to say the words just yet, but I could definitely show him what he meant to me. The decision about visiting the demon realm could wait because I had a marshmallow of a demon to devour.

16 | AZAZEL

I WAS AN IDIOT. In my attempt to figure out a way to broach the subject with Elijah—or even if I wanted to do it in the first place—I'd failed to see what my indecision was doing to him.

I couldn't believe he'd thought I was going to leave, but then again, he was used to it, wasn't he? Getting left behind? He had abandonment issues, and I'd just compounded them with my own idiocy.

As if that wasn't enough, I'd then made him feel like I didn't want him to see my home. If I could, I'd share every part of my life with him. But he didn't know that.

"Do you want to?" I asked as I pulled back so he could breathe. I could never forget he was human, especially in moments like these when his heart beat faster because of me. "Visit the demon realm, I mean."

After Elijah demanded his answers, we'd devoured the lunch I'd had delivered, and then gone right back to kissing. But now, I needed to know what was going through his head.

Elijah blinked rapidly, clearing the haze from his eyes as he licked his lips. I felt something like pride wash through me at having affected him so much, and I couldn't resist tracing his wet lower lip with my thumb.

He bit the pad of my thumb, winking as he settled into my lap once more, his arms thrown over my shoulders this time. It didn't look like the most comfortable position, but he didn't seem to care.

"I'd love to see your home Az. You know that. But if you really don't want me there, it's okay. I respect your choices."

I shook my head, dipping my head so he wouldn't see all the way into my soul with those penetrating eyes of his. "I'd like you to see it. But I don't know if it'll work. Please don't be disappointed if it doesn't."

Elijah tipped my head up, a smile on his lips that he pressed to the tip of my nose. "I won't. As long as I have you, everything else is just a bonus."

Butterflies fluttered in my belly at his words, and I was glad no one could hear my thoughts because they'd taken an utterly disgusting sappy turn.

"You have the weekend off, don't you? We'll go then," I decided, and he grinned.

"Perfect." He glanced at the clock before turning to me, brow raised.

"We have time before dinner. What do you wanna do?" His fingers trailed down my side, blazing a path over my skin and telling me what he would like.

I bit my lip, unsure. I wanted to give Elijah what he wanted, and if he'd asked for it verbally, I'd have been compelled to give it to him, but he hadn't. And he'd told me he never wanted me to do anything I didn't want to.

Over the past six months, there had been many instances where I'd had to remind myself of that.

"How about a movie and some cuddle time?" I suggested carefully, and instead of looking disappointed, he merely smiled widely and leaned back to grab the remote from the coffee table.

"Sounds good. But I'll choose the movie this time," he declared, and I had no problem with that because I felt more content and happy than I ever had. I'd never had a summoner who was anywhere as good as Elijah, and I thanked Fate or whoever was responsible for bringing Elijah into my life.

Once he'd started the movie, an action flick that I knew he loved, he made me lie down on the couch before snuggling into my front. His head rested on my arm, and I wrapped the other one around his waist, pulling him into me. He sighed happily, and the sound warmed my chest.

I knew our time together was limited, so I intended to cherish every single moment. Years from now, I wanted to be able to remember the sweet, strawberry scent of his shampoo and the underlying scent of him. I wanted to remember how he felt in my arms, what his smile looked like. How his smile made me feel.

I didn't want to think about how painful our separation would be because I knew it would be soul-shattering. I'd never felt like this about anyone, and a part of me wished Elijah was a demon because then at least there would be a possibility he was my mate.

But would Elijah be Elijah if he was a demon? Would he be the same sassy, brave man?

I shook off the thought, knowing it didn't matter. It didn't matter what Elijah was because I'd love him in any form. It didn't matter that he wasn't my mate because I still loved him with my whole soul.

"That was fun, wasn't it? Do you want to watch the second one?"

I blinked back to the present, surprised the movie had ended already. I didn't want to stop holding Elijah, didn't want to let this moment end, so I nodded, pressing a kiss to the top of his head. "Let's watch another one."

He grinned, smacked a kiss on my chin, and turned back to the screen, his copper curls brushing against my skin.

Who would have thought someone like me could love someone like Elijah? Hell, who would have thought I could love at all?

I was a demon, and I'd been created for violence, torture, and mayhem. But maybe, maybe demons were evolving now that violence wasn't a part of our life anymore. Maybe this was proof that we could change too. That we could feel.

Demons were allowed to move to Afterworld. That wouldn't be possible if they thought we were evil, would it?

Not a lot of demons had accepted that invitation, though that was mostly because they were skeptical.

Maybe I'd give it a try, after my time with Elijah ended. The thought of going back to live in the demon world didn't appeal to me much, and I didn't think I'd be able to bear being around Elijah without touching him or watch him move on with someone else, someone human who could give him the life he deserved.

Elijah wrapped his hand around me, placing our joined hands on his chest. The small movement pulled me away from my unhappy thoughts, and I drew him closer to me, focusing on the present. The future could wait.

17 | ELIJAH

"Ready?" Az asked, and I smiled up at me. Out of the two of us, he was clearly more nervous, but I humored him, squeezing his hand in assurance.

"I'm ready, Az. I want to see your home."

He smiled once and dipped his head, his hand tightening around mine. "Ask me to take you."

"Azazel, take me to the demon realm," I said, trying to sound as commanding as I could. Az grinned, telling me I hadn't quite succeeded.

"Yes, master," he replied, voice teasing, and waved his hand. Magic stirred in the air, and wind whipped around us as the floor started shaking beneath us. I looked down as a crack spread across the floor, and a gasp slipped past my lips a moment before we fell in.

I snapped my eyes shut as we fell, feeling like I'd left my stomach somewhere in my room. My hand clung to Az's with a punishing grip, and I would've wrapped myself around him if I could've.

I wasn't sure how long we fell, but after a while, my feet finally touched solid ground again. I still waited until my legs felt steady enough before I opened my eyes, a gasp slipping past my lips as I looked around.

Whatever I'd been expecting the demon realm to look like, it hadn't been this. We were clearly in Azazel's living space, and it looked almost...normal. Except for the fact that there were no windows and the flame in the fireplace was blue.

Az's space was made up of one large room divided into a lounge area and a bedroom, with a large couch on one side of the room, and a bed double the size of mine on the other. He had books piled beside the couch, and a dog bed rested beside his bed, probably for his demonhound friend, Hella.

The walls were made of black stone, and they were a few shades darker than Az's skin. Lanterns hung from the ceiling, lit with similar blue fire.

"Why is the fire blue?" I asked, and Az, who I now realized had been nervously watching me study his room, raised a brow at me.

"That's your first question?"

"Yup," I said, popping the 'p' as I walked over to the couch to check out his collection of books.

"Before, the Burning Chasm and the demon realm were connected, so we shared the same fire. When the entrance to the Chasm was closed off, we lost access. I guess the magic of the realms decided we could do with a color change. Also, this fire isn't really hot. It just gives light," Az explained, and I changed course to head to the fireplace instead.

I leaned close to the flames and realized he was right. The flames weren't hot at all, but they weren't cold either. Experimentally, I stuck the tip of my index finger into the flame and grinned when all I felt was a slight tickling sensation.

"That is so cool," I exclaimed, and Az bit his lip, looking curious.

"It is?"

"Absolutely!" Returning to my original destination, I picked up the first book in the stack, running my finger over the leather cover. The book was thick, and it looked old. Very old.

I carefully opened it, aware of Azazel watching me quietly, and realized the book was in a language I didn't know. I tilted my head, flipping through a few pages before looking up at Az.

"What language is this?"

"It's Russian."

I blinked in surprise, glancing from him to the book and back again. "You know Russian?"

"I know all the languages, little human. I've been around for a while, remember? One of the oldest demons here was Russian when he was in the human realm. He wrote stories about his life, his time, so he wouldn't forget. A lot of demons did that in the early days, so they had something that would help them remember who they were and not get lost in the darkness of the dark souls they punished. Now, we read them for fun."

"Wow," I murmured, running my finger over a drawing of a flower. The ink was old, as was the paper, and the nerdy part of me wished I could read it. "Any of these in English?"

Az made a humming sound before kneeling beside the stack, shuffling through a few books before he found the one he was looking for. It looked a little newer than the Russian one, but still quite old. The leather was a dark brown color, with a symbol carved into it.

"Here. It's the only one, but it's not a fun read. The demon who wrote it moved on to Afterworld a while ago, but he wrote a lot about the souls he tortured. Their stories, their sins."

Curious, I flipped the book open, cringing as it opened on a page with a very detailed drawing of a man ripping a heart out of a woman's chest.

"Oh, and he was very good at art too," Az added as he stood up, his eyes falling to the page I'd opened. He winced. "Like I said, not a fun read."

After seeing a few more of the drawings, I decided the book definitely wasn't for me. Placing it back on the shelf, I sat down on the couch, looking up at Azazel. "So, it worked. I asked you to bring me to the demon realm, and you did it. Why do you think no other summoner ever asked their demon to bring them here?" I mused, and Azazel got a look on his face that I couldn't quite read.

I shifted closer to him as he settled on the couch, turning a little so I could see him better. He met my eyes, his red ones flickering in the lantern light as he took my hand in his, brushing his thumb over my knuckles.

"It's probably because in this realm, the demon isn't bound to his summoner anymore."

18 | AZAZEL

It took Elijah a moment to understand the implications of what I'd said, and his eyes widened when it finally clicked, though he didn't pull his hand away from me.

"So, you're not bound to me anymore?" he asked, and I detected a hint of sadness in his tone. As well as I knew him, I knew he wasn't sad because he couldn't control me anymore, but just because he didn't want to lose the bond we shared.

"We still have a bond. You're still the human who summoned me. But here, I don't feel the same compulsion to follow your orders," I explained, and he tilted his head, looking thoughtful.

"Do a headstand," he told me, and I grinned when it did absolutely nothing. I could ignore it without a sweat. "Fuck, this is awesome. We should just stay here."

I raised a brow, waving around the fire-lit cave we were in. "You want to live in a cave instead of your nice, airy apartment?"

Elijah made a face, shaking his head. "I know, I know. It sounds crazy. But this place is kinda cozy. And I like that I can't control you anymore. It means that all of this," he waved between us, "is really real."

I rolled my eyes. "It's always been real, little human. You didn't force me to want you. Trust me."

Elijah smiled, clearly pleased, and eyed the exit of my cave. "Can we go outside? Can I see more of the realm?"

I blew out a breath, thinking about it. While the other demons wouldn't exactly attack Elijah, I wasn't sure what their reaction would be. As far as I remembered, it hadn't ever happened before.

"I just realized...there's no food in this realm, is there?" Elijah asked, looking far too dejected by the prospect. Had he really been serious about wanting to stay in the demon realm forever?

I waved my hand, and magic stirred in the air before a packet of crisps fell into Elijah's lap. "I wouldn't usually be able to do that, but our bond lets me use you as a sort of conduit to the human realm."

Elijah picked up the packet, eyeing it curiously. "So did you magic this or steal it from the human realm?"

"Why don't you eat the crisps and let me worry about where they came from?" I asked with a wink, and Elijah shook his head before opening the packet and stuffing a few crisps into his mouth.

"Now, do I get to see more of the demon realm?" he asked, eyes alight with curiosity.

"You know that human saying? Curiosity killed the cat?" I asked, and Elijah waved me off.

"I'm not worried about that."

"And why not, if I may ask?" I raised a brow at him, leaning against the stone wall as I watched him.

He grinned at me, pushing his glasses up his nose. "Because I know you'll keep me safe."

What was that feeling in my chest? It was warm and gooey and icky. It made me want to pull Elijah into a tight hug and never let go.

Shaking my head, I straightened up and offered my palm to Elijah. Grinning, he took it and hopped to his feet, sticking close to my side as I led the way out of my cave and into the main tunnel that ran through the whole realm.

The demon realm wasn't all that big, and the tunnel connected all the caves in the realm. Lamps hung on both sides, lighting up the path in a blue glow, and Elijah's eyes tracked each lamp, glowing with curiosity as he studied them.

"There's not much to see in the realm, to be honest. Most caves are like mine, belonging to a demon. There are around 150 demons here, though the numbers go down every decade as more of us decide its time to move on," I explained, and Elijah looked up at me, amber eyes glowing strangely in the blue light.

"Have you thought about it? Moving on?"

I shrugged, not willing to admit that I had. "I like the human realm too much to want to move on," I settled on saying, which wasn't a complete lie. I did like the human realm, but not because of all the art and food, like I did before. Now, I liked the human realm for just one reason: Elijah.

"Would you like to meet a friend of mine?" I asked, spotting Fressia's cave up ahead. We hadn't been spotted by a demon yet, and I figured Fressia would be the safest demon to introduce Elijah to, since she already knew about him.

"A demon friend?" Elijah asked, his eyes going wide behind his glasses, and I chuckled softly.

"Yes, a demon friend. Her name is Fressia."

Elijah nodded after a moment of stunned silence, and I stopped in front of Fressia's cave, knowing she'd sense my presence.

"Az, you brought a guest! Come on in," she called, and Elijah shot me a wide-eyed look as I parted the curtains and waited for Elijah to step into the cave before following him inside.

My human froze the moment he spotted Fressia, his eyes widening as he took her in. Should I have told him a little about her before bringing him here? He looked stunned speechless, and his lips parted.

Fressia, being the mischievous demon she was, threw her deep red hair over her shoulder and moved toward Elijah, caressing his legs with the end of her tail and making him jump.

"Fressia," I warned, and she shot me a grin.

"You didn't tell me how pretty your human was, Azzy," she said, and I glared at her, both as a reminder that Elijah was *mine*, and because of the stupid nickname.

"You have beautiful eyes," Elijah said, finally finding his voice, and I glared harder at her, as if it was her fault Elijah liked her eyes. She simply ignored me, giving Elijah her full attention.

"So do you. Elijah, right? I'm Fressia. Nice to meet you. I've heard a *lot* about you," she said, offering her hand, and Elijah shook it, giving her a curious look.

"You have?" he asked, and Fressia shot me a grin before speaking.

"Aye. All this big lug has talked about recently is you. It's kinda adorable, actually," she said, and I scowled at her.

The fond expression Elijah gave me soothed me some, though, and I let them talk about me like I wasn't standing right there just because of how happy it made Elijah.

Fucking hell, when had he turned me into this lovesick puppy?

19 | ELIJAH

THE STORIES FRESSIA TOLD me about Azazel sounded nothing like the guy I knew, but they were a reminder that Az wasn't simply a guy; he was a demon who'd once punished and tortured evil souls in these caves.

"Do you know the story of how Az lost his horns?" Fressia asked, and I shook my head. She was seated on a plush, deep red couch across from us, and she looked like a work of art, with her red scales gleaming in the light from the fire and her red hair stark against the pale skin of her upper body. She was naked like Az had been when I'd first summoned him—he now wore pants in both forms for my sake—but scales covered most of her front like a pseudo-shirt, ending just above her chest.

"I swear to Afterworld, Fressia," Azazel growled, but she waved him off.

"So, once upon a time, Az was given the job of torturing a soul. This was when Underworld was still working, obviously, and the souls we got ranged from evil to simply desperate. Now, the souls who'd committed crimes out of desperation usually end up in Otherworld and get a chance to redeem themselves, but back then, they all ended up here."

I nodded along as Az huffed beside me. He'd told me all about Otherworld and how the realms worked. I wasn't supposed to know all this, but then again, I wasn't supposed to have a demon lover either.

"So, the soul Az was intended to torture had held up a bank at gunpoint and robbed it. He'd done it to save his son's life, to pay medical bills, I think. But he'd accidentally shot a man, so when he died, he ended up here for his crimes. Now, Az, being the sweetheart he was, didn't torture him the way he was supposed to because he felt sorry for the man."

"Oh no," I murmured, sensing where this was going as I remembered what Az had told me way back when I'd first summoned him, when I'd asked him why his horns were chopped off.

"Oh yes. The elder demons decided Az wasn't doing his job properly and that he'd earned a punishment. Those old fuckers chopped his horns off as a reminder to all demons to take their jobs 'seriously.' Joke's on them, though, because a decade later Underworld closed up, and the Burning Chasm took its place, leaving us with no souls to torment."

"You know what the best part was?" Az asked, and I raised a brow at him.

"There's a best part to all of this?"

He nodded, a vindicated smile on his face. "Every last one of the elder demons ended up in the Chasm."

"What? How?" I asked, confused. I'd assumed only the evil souls went into the Burning Chasm. Then again, someone who'd cut off Az's horns had to have at least some evil in them.

"It's a known fact that constant proximity to evil souls can...infect you, I suppose is the right word. It was why Underworld was shut down in the first place. The souls were turning the demons darker, turning them into creatures that thrived on torture and punishment. Most of the older demons ended up in the Chasm, and the ones that remain here now are the youngest of the demons," Fressia explained, and I shook my head in wonder.

It was hard to imagine not knowing all of this now, but until a few months ago, I'd had no idea there were other beings out there, let alone other realms. I felt a little sorry for all the humans who had no clue they lived in a world full of magic.

"That's good. I'm glad they were punished for what they did to you," I told Az, and Fressia grinned widely.

"Aww, you two are just adorable. I can see now why Azzy is so head over heels for you," she said, and I rolled my eyes, waving her off even as my cheeks flamed.

Azazel growled softly, but it only made her chuckle. It was clear to me that they were good friends, and I was once again glad I'd asked Az to bring me here. Getting a glimpse of his home and his life here was wonderful, and it made me appreciate having him with me even more.

"Oh, Az. Have you heard about the things going on in Otherworld?" Fressia asked, and I tuned back into the conversation as Az frowned, shaking his head.

"What's going on?"

"There seems to be some kind of trouble down in the Chasm. I heard through a soul collector they put up new warding around it. They don't know all the details yet, but something big is going down. I'm sure of that."

"Maybe there was another breakout attempt?" Az mused, and I raised a brow at him.

"From the Chasm? Like the torture place of all the evil souls?" I demanded, and Az nodded.

"There was a breakout a few years ago, but the King of Otherworld stopped it before the souls could escape Otherworld."

I blinked, trying to imagine what would happen if there was another, if the souls found their way to the human realm. Would they destroy it? Try to take over? Kill everyone? I shuddered just thinking about it, and I had to shake my head to get rid of the images.

"Whatever's happening, I'm sure the Otherworlders will take care of it. They always do," Fressia said, and Az hummed.

"That's true. Elijah, I think it's time we return home. What do you say?"

I had absolutely no idea what hour it was, or how much time had passed since we came here, but if Az thought it was time, I had no reason to doubt him.

"Sounds good," I told him before turning to Fressia. "It was nice meeting you."

"You too, sweetie. Keep this lug on his toes, you hear?"

I chuckled as I nodded, and Az just shook his head before tugging me out of her room and back down the tunnel to his room.

"Wait, wait, don't take us back yet," I said when we were in his room, and he gave me a curious look, stopping in the middle of his cave.

"Why not?"

"Because I need to do this first," I said before pushing up on my toes and pressing my lips to his.

20 | Azazel

A week after our visit to the demon realm, there was a knock at our door at ten in the evening.

Elijah and I shared a glance. We both knew we weren't expecting anyone, and that put me on high alert. I shifted to my human form before walking over to the door, motioning for Elijah to stay behind.

My little human ignored me as usual, of course, and slid up beside me as I opened the door.

We both stared at the woman standing on the other side. She was dark-skinned, dressed in jeans and a white t-shirt. Her arms were covered in tattoos in a brilliant shade of red. She would've seemed like a stranger if not for the very familiar red hair and yellow eyes she sported.

"Fressia?" Elijah asked before I could, and she smiled widely at him.

"Hey, Elijah! You gonna invite me in?" she asked, and Elijah smacked my arm, tugging me backward. Since I was in my human form, he actually managed to pull me back.

"Let her in, Az," he said, and I grudgingly opened the door wider. Even though she was my friend, I didn't know if I was comfortable letting another demon into our home. If she was here, that meant she had been summoned. And who knew what her summoner wanted from us?

"Get that constipated look off your face, Az. No one sent me here," Fressia said, tossing her hair back as she settled on the couch as if this was her house. I bit back a growl as I stuck close to Elijah, who didn't seem to mind having a second demon in his home.

"Can I get you a drink, Fressia?" Elijah asked, and she smiled widely.

"You're such a sweetie. I'd love a cup of coffee," she said, and I stopped Elijah when he started moving toward the kitchen.

"Tell us what you're doing here first, and then you can have some coffee," I challenged her, and she grinned, completely unruffled.

"If it will make you a little less growly, sure. The king of Otherworld vacated the demon realm. All the demons are now here in the human realm," she said, and I stared at her, sure she was joking.

"Really?" Elijah demanded, much more willing to trust her than I was, even though I'd known her longer.

"Yes. The queen of Underworld is trying to break out of the Chasm, apparently, and they were worried she'll try to do it through the demon realm. Then Mammon got himself summoned by one of the dark souls. They practically shit themselves trying to get us out of there before the dark souls could summon any more," Fressia explained, and her tale sounded more unrealistic the more she spoke.

"I don't believe you," I told her, and she rolled her yellow eyes.

"I don't care. All the demons are under strict orders to not hurt any humans and to look out for any escaped dark souls. Figured I'd let you know," she said, twirling her dark hair around her finger.

"Who summoned you?" I asked, and she bit her lip.

"I can't tell you that," she said, and I realized it was a term of her contract. "But," she added with a mischievous smile, "I can mention the completely unrelated fact that it's someone I just talked about."

I raised a brow at her, going back through our conversation before my eyes widened. The fucking king of Otherworld had summoned her? But how?

Shaking my head, I decided I wasn't going to try to wrap my head around that one. "So what are you doing here? Don't you have orders about where to be?"

"Not really. As long as I look out for dark souls and don't hurt humans, I can do whatever I want," she said with a wide smile, and for the first time, I took in how happy she looked, how excited.

"Well, I'm happy for you, then. But don't turn up here unannounced or I'll fry you to the bones," I threatened.

"Azazel!" Elijah gasped, looking horrified that I'd threatened her, but Fressia merely laughed.

"Understood, Azzy. I'm going to take off while I still can. Be on the lookout for dark souls and take care of this cutie," she said, winking at Elijah as I growled. I couldn't help myself. My human brought out a jealousy in me that I'd never felt before.

Once Fressia was gone, I pulled Elijah to me and hugged him tightly, shifting back to my true form so I could properly hold him.

"Do the dark souls have any reason to come looking for us?" Elijah asked, his cheek pressed firmly against my chest.

"Not really. I think she just wanted us to stay on guard because the Otherworld king told her to be. If the dark souls do come to the human realm, they'll probably go into hiding until they're no longer a priority to the Otherworlders," I said. I'd known Mammon. Once upon a time, he'd been my mentor. I knew the way he thought, and I knew he wasn't above manipulating the person who summoned him into doing whatever was the best for him.

"We'll be careful, then," he said, and I smiled softly as I looked down at my human. He was such a fierce little creature.

Reaching down, I cupped his chin in my palm, tipping it up so I could look into his eyes. "Yes, we will. I won't let anyone hurt you," I promised, and Elijah smiled before rising up on his toes, his intention clear. I grabbed him around the waist, pulling him into the air and making him laugh.

His laughter subsided as he placed his palms on my cheeks and claimed my lips with his. I hummed into the kiss, pulling him closer as I stuck my tongue into his mouth. No matter how many times I kissed Elijah, it was never enough. It would never be enough.

21 | ELIJAH

"You know, every time I attend his lecture, I wonder if Mr. Rivers even knows anything about computers," I grumbled as I unlocked the door to our apartment, turning to look at Az as I opened the door.

"What's wrong with you today? You've been scarily quie—" I froze as I turned back around, blinking stupidly at the scene before me. Fairy lights decorated the walls of our living room, the couch was covered in soft, fluffy blankets, boxes of pizzas were stacked on the coffee table, and the TV was turned on, just waiting for someone to pick a show and start watching.

"Az..." I murmured, turning to him. He scratched the back of his neck, looking everywhere but at me. "You did this?" I murmured, more of a statement than a question. Who else would do something so sweet for me?

"You've been having a rough few days at school, so I thought I'd do something for you," Az said with a shrug, as if it was no big deal.

Dropping my bag on the floor, I wrapped my arms around him, burying my face in the crook of his neck. He hadn't changed back to his true form since the door wasn't fully closed, and we were almost the same height like this. I breathed in his familiar smoky scent and thanked whatever deity had led me to finding that summoning spell that day.

No one had ever cared for me the way Az did, and I never, ever wanted to lose him. The reminder that I only had a few more months left before our one-year deal ended popped up in my head, but I pushed it back, not wanting anything to ruin the cozy evening Az had arranged for us.

"So, what are we watching?" I asked, pulling back just enough that I could push the door closed. The moment the door clicked shut, I felt Az ripple under my touch, and the next moment, he was back to his true form. After a lot of kissing and words of appreciation, I'd finally managed to convince him that I loved everything about this form of his.

"Whatever you want," Az said, his red eyes glowing warmly.

I grinned at that, and I felt a little bad for taking advantage of it when he'd given me such a nice surprise, but I couldn't help fucking with him a little. It was practically our love language by now.

"How about *Beauty and the Beast*?" I suggested, and the scowl was instant. I'd discovered some months ago that Az had an unexplainable hate for all things Disney. He still hadn't told me why, but I was determined to needle him until he did.

"Why would you want to watch that when you're living it?" he asked, and I rolled my eyes at him.

"Of course. How could I forget I have my own big, bad beast?" I said mock-seriously, and Az narrowed his eyes at me.

"If you don't straighten up, I'm going to magick all of this away," he threatened, though I was sure it was an empty threat. Mostly sure.

"Okay, okay. How about that show we added to our watch-list last month? The rom-com," I suggested, and Az nodded.

Ten minutes later, I'd washed up and changed into comfier clothes—one major bonus of having a demon boyfriend who could magick anything for you was having the best, comfiest clothes you could want—I joined Az on the couch, cuddling into his side as he covered us with the soft-as-sin blanket that definitely wasn't from my closet.

As Azazel navigated through the options on the TV to find the show I'd mentioned, I took a moment to just observe him. He was so beautiful, his dark skin glowing and his tight curls gleaming like he wore a crown from all the fairy lights, his lips pursed as he searched for the show. I may have called him my big, bad beast, but he was a lot more like Prince Charming to me. He'd turned my life around, replaced my loneliness with a contentment I'd never felt before.

"I love you," I said, voice soft, just as the show's theme began playing, and I froze as Az's head snapped to me, his eyes wide.

"What did you say?" he asked, voice equally soft, and I debated whether or not to tell him for a full second before deciding I'd hidden my feelings long enough.

"I love you, Az," I repeated, my voice a lot stronger this time. I shifted closer to him, pressing my palm on his chest. "And it's okay if you don't feel the same. I just—I wanted you to know."

"Not feel the same? Elijah, I feel like I've always loved you," Az said, his voice warm and dripping with sincerity. It was my turn to look at him in shock, and he smiled softly. "I knew it the day you told me you wanted to see my home, the day you let me pick cuddles and a movie over sex."

That...that had been a few months ago. Wow.

"It was basic human decency, Az. The second part, I mean," I said, wishing he hadn't lived a life where that made me special to him.

"I guess then I haven't met many decent humans," he said with a shrug, and that made me worry. What if he only thought he loved me because I was the only human who'd ever been nice to him?

"Stop. I can practically see your thought process," Az growled, and I ducked my head. "I love you for who you are, and yes, that includes your kindness, but it's not the only reason. Okay?"

I nodded, accepting him at his word simply because he had no reason to lie.

"Good, now let's watch this show before the pizza gets cold," Az declared, and I smiled as I cuddled into him, his words settling warmly in my chest.

22 | ELIJAH

I BLINKED AT MY Kindle as the words started mushing together and realized it might be time I turned it off and slept. Az had fallen asleep almost an hour ago, his body a familiar warmth at my side.

Placing the Kindle on my nightstand, I turned on my side so I was facing him, his arm shifting around my waist before wrapping more securely around me. Smiling, I snuggled closer to him, sliding my arm over his hip to hold him to me.

My eyelids fluttered shut, and I exhaled deeply before dragging in Az's fire-and-smoke scent. Just as I was about to fall asleep, Az's arm tightened around me.

Pulling my head back, I looked up at him, brows furrowed. "Az? You okay?"

Az stayed quiet, apparently still asleep, but his arm didn't loosen its grip around me. He bent his head, burying his nose into my hair and breathing deeply, as if scenting me. Unsure what to do, I held him in return and let him wrap himself around me.

Azazel was so lighthearted and fun-filled most of the time that I sometimes forgot he'd practically lived in Hell for most of his life. I couldn't even begin to imagine the shit he'd seen, and I was sure he'd never actually had a chance to process that.

I'd seen a therapist every few days for six months after my father was arrested, and I still saw her sometimes when I was having an especially bad week. Who was Az supposed to talk to, if he even wanted to? A human therapist would just get him sent to the loony bin.

That was a worry for later, though. Right now, all I needed to do was hold Az and help him through whatever nightmare was haunting him.

"Shhh, you're okay, Az. You're okay," I murmured, rubbing his back as I held him close.

After a long while, he relaxed in my hold, and after some time I finally fell asleep, but when I woke the next morning, I remembered what had happened, even if Az didn't. Az didn't usually show me his vulnerable side, but he had last night, and I didn't quite know if I should mention it to him or not.

"Good morning, Az," I greeted him as I walked into the kitchen. He was standing beside the coffee machine, waiting for it to finish brewing. It was a ritual he'd adopted soon after he came here, just like 90 percent of America's adult and young adult population.

"No," Az grumbled, and I bit back a smile.

"I think the appropriate response to that is good morning," I said, just to fuck with him, and he gave me a squinty-eyed look.

"No."

"Yes, but—"

"No."

I chuckled, and he scowled at me. We may or may not have finished a six-pack of beer last night. Neither of us were big drinkers, and while I'd stopped after my second one, Az had finished four all on his own, and he was clearly feeling the effects. He wouldn't have if I hadn't specifically asked him to get drunk on the beer—on his request—and while he'd thoroughly enjoyed the feeling of being drunk, I was pretty sure he wasn't enjoying the aftereffects.

"Can't you, like, magic away your hangover?" I asked, and he raised a brow at me, as if the answer was obvious.

Considering how it'd been ten months since I summoned him—a fact I avoided thinking about whenever I could—and it was something that always made my blood boil, I was surprised I hadn't realized it already. Maybe I was still a little drunk.

"Shit. Want me to take care of it?" I asked, and he shot me the stink-eye.

"Do you want me to beg?"

"Jeez. Chill out, man. Az, please use your magic to get rid of your hangover," I said, and he sighed, snapping his fingers.

"Better?" I asked with a grin, and he nodded.

"Much."

The coffee machine beeped, and he filled two mugs before walking over to me and handing one to me.

"Are you okay?" I asked after I'd taken a sip of the perfectly brewed coffee.

"Yeah, it was just a hangover. I'm fine," he said. Clearly, he didn't remember last night. Or maybe he just didn't want to mention his bad dream to me. Should I push?

"Uh, last night, did you have a nightmare?" I asked, deciding to fuck it. Az had helped me with so many of my issues, and I wanted him to feel like he could talk to me if he wanted to.

Az furrowed his brows, as if thinking about it, and then sucked in a sharp breath, going stock-still. After a moment, he shook his head and shot me a cocky grin, though I could see the lingering unease in his eyes.

"I don't have nightmares, Eli. Though I have starred in a lot of them."

I rolled my eyes and lightly slapped his massive chest. "I'm trying to have a serious conversation with you!"

"And I'm trying to subtly avoid it," he growled back.

"Well, that wasn't very subtle," I said with a grin, and he huffed, gulping down the steaming coffee like it was nothing. "You can talk to me, you know," I said, softening my voice as I placed my palm on his chest right over his heart.

Bright red eyes met mine as he covered my palm with his, his chest rising and falling in even breaths even though he technically didn't need to breathe.

"I know. It was nothing, I promise. Just a stupid dream. I'm a demon, Eli. The stuff from Underworld doesn't bother me like you think it does. I wasn't made that way," Az said, and I believed him even if some part of me insisted that couldn't be true. But it made sense, didn't it? Az was supposed to punish the evil souls, not suffer himself, so why would their wrong-doings affect him?

But if it wasn't that, what was it?

Az sighed and shifted his eyes to the floor between us. "I can see you don't plan on letting this go."

I shrugged, and he glared at me.

"Fine. I dreamed about losing you, okay?" he snapped before grabbing his mug and stalking over to the sink. He slammed the mug a little too hard, and I jumped. He didn't turn around, but I could see how tightly he was holding on to the sink. Shit, maybe I shouldn't have pushed him.

Quietly, I walked over to him and wrapped my arms around him from behind, pressing my face into the space between and below his shoulder blades. His skin was blazing hot as always, and I whispered against it, "I have nightmares about losing you too."

Azazel didn't react for a long moment, and I held on to him, waiting him out. Then, he jerked around and pulled me to him, his lips crashing into mine as he kissed me like his life depended on it.

23 | Azazel

Demons didn't really have a lot of feelings. It wasn't that we were unfeeling robots, but more that our emotions were dampened so we could do our jobs properly when Underworld still existed.

I'd only just started truly experiencing emotions in all their depths since bonding with Elijah, but the one emotion I still couldn't figure out how to deal with was the one haunting me the most these days: fear.

I'd never been afraid before, but the closer we drew to the end of our contract, the more I felt it clawing at me. I didn't want to leave my little human, but I also didn't know what else to do.

I had a feeling the answer was just out of reach, that if I could just get a handle on my fear I'd figure it out, but so far, I'd had no luck.

He was at school, and I'd—probably for the first time since I started joining him—stayed back because I knew he could sense something was up with me, but I hadn't wanted to confess exactly what.

"Who killed *your* dog?"

I jumped to my feet, growling when I realized it was just Fressia. "What the fuck, Fres!"

She widened her eyes in mock-fear, raising her palms up in surrender. "Whoa. Did you and your little human get in a fight or something?"

"No," I snapped, and she walked over to me, her ruby red heels clicking against the floor. She settled on the couch beside me, throwing one leg over the other as she turned to face me.

"Talk to me," she said, losing the sharp edge to her voice that she usually donned like armor.

Sighing, I rubbed my palm over my face. "Our contract ends in less than a month."

Fressia stared at me for a long moment, as if waiting for me to continue. When I didn't say anything, her brows shot up. "Wait. That's it? That's what got your panties in a twist?"

I growled at her since I couldn't find the words to express how annoying I found her. She shook her head as if she was disappointed in me, and then said, "Wow, you're dumber than I thought."

I aimed a smack at her, and she dodged it easily before pulling me into a headlock. "Fuck, Fres. Let go!"

"Not until I knock some sense into you. Such a big head and it's all empty in there, isn't it?" she teased, her arm loosening just a bit.

"I'm not stupid," I protested, and she scoffed.

"Sure, if you say so. What's your explanation for not having figured this out? It's not that hard."

"I don't know what to do. It's not like Eli can just summon me again," I grumbled, and she dropped her arm and gave me a look of disbelief.

"Who told you that?" she asked incredulously, and I got a sinking feeling deep in my gut.

"Uh, Ryk," I said, and she rolled her eyes.

"Are you kidding me? You believed Ryk? He's a sweetheart, but he's even dumber than you. Then again, you were dumb enough to believe him, so who knows?"

"Will you please stop calling me dumb?" I growled as I processed what she was saying. Did she mean what I thought?

"So what you're saying is Elijah can summon me again?"

"Duh. As long as he has the spell, sure. That thing about not being able to summon a demon twice? That's from the old days. Back then, demons got summoned so they could corrupt souls and get more of them into Underworld because torturing them was their idea of fun. When the rules changed, that rule was changed too. Maybe this time you could ask him to make a better contract. Like a lifetime one, maybe?" she suggested with a waggle of her brows.

"I can ask him to summon me again," I repeated quietly, and maybe I was a dumbass because the thought hadn't even crossed my mind. Of course, part of it was because I'd believed Ryk, but still. I should've known better.

"Really hard not to call you dumb when you're acting like it," Fressia said with a frown, and this time I landed a smack on her arm. Rolling her eyes, she brushed off her arm, as if rubbing off my touch. "If you're done with your pity party, I want to tell you the thing I came here to tell you."

"What is it?" I asked as a feeling of relief settled into my chest. I wouldn't have to leave Elijah.

"You know how I told you the Otherworld rulers summoned all the demons to get them to the human realm?"

"Yeah, you told me last time. Because the demon realm wasn't secure, right?" I asked, and she nodded.

"They've resolved the issue, but some of the dark souls managed to get to the human realm with Mammon's help." Mammon was one of the oldest demons that existed, and I wasn't surprised that he'd bonded to a dark soul.

"That sucks. Mammon is pretty powerful. Those dark souls could cause some serious damage with him," I said, and Fressia nodded, her lips turning down in a frown.

"Yeah. It's why the Otherworld rulers have ordered us to stay in the human realm—not that we mind, of course—and find those souls and Mammon. All of us are spread out over the country and doing whatever we can to find them, though we haven't had any luck so far."

"Do you need my help?" I asked, and she smiled, patting my arm.

"Nah, you have fun with your human. If I do, I will ask for it. I promise."

I nodded and glanced over at the clock, realizing Eli would be back soon. I couldn't wait to tell him what Fressia had told me.

"I can see I'm losing you, so one last thing and then I'm gone," Fressia said, and I turned my attention back to her. "So, Ryk, Nico, and Star are sharing a four-bedroom apartment with a human."

"Holy shit. Really?"

Fressia laughed, her head bobbing up and down. "Oh yeah. The poor kid is probably at his wit's end about what to do with them. He obviously doesn't know what they are, but you know how Ryk and Star can be."

"Yeah, I'm having trouble imagining them trying to act human," I said with a shake of my head, and she grinned.

"It's better than any show Netflix has to offer."

"I bet," I said, sneaking a glance at the clock again. Fressia wasn't easy to fool, though, and she caught me instantly. She gave a short laugh before standing, her red hair falling forward as she patted my cheek.

"Be good to your human. I'll see you later." As suddenly as she'd appeared, she was gone.

I sat back on the couch as energy thrummed under my skin and started counting down the minutes until Eli would be home.

24 | ELIJAH

I was so tired it felt like my backpack was full of rocks. The moment I got into the apartment, I was going to drag Az into bed and cuddle him for an hour straight.

One moment I was stepping through my door, and the next I was surrounded by a firm, warm body that smelled of smoke. Az. I relaxed into his hold, and he held on to me tighter, his face pressed into my curls, his arms like bands of steel around me.

I kicked the door shut without trying to move out of his arms. The last thing we needed was for someone to see him in his true form. Then again, we'd probably be able to pass it off as some really good cosplay getup. Humans were easy to fool.

When Az kept holding me, I realized this wasn't a usual "I'm glad you're home" hug.

"Az? Is everything okay?"

Finally, he pulled back, and I looked up into his red eyes, searching for any clues about what had happened.

"Everything's perfect. I...I figured it out," he said, and it didn't take me more than a second to realize what he meant.

"You won't have to leave?" I asked, and he shook his head. A wide smile spread across my lips, and I pulled him to me. He came willingly, and I pressed my lips to his, hoping he could feel all my love, hoping he knew how fucking glad I was that he'd figured it out.

If we hadn't figured it out, I was thinking about asking him to take me to the demon world with him. I didn't know if I would've been kicked out once our bond ended, but I figured it was a chance I had to take.

"So? What do we have to do?" I asked, pulling back just enough to meet his eyes.

"You have to summon me again," he said, and I blinked.

"Oh," I murmured, and his smile dimmed.

"Unless you don't want to. I just assumed...but it's okay if you don't—" I pressed my fingers to his lips, stopping his rambling.

"Shut up, Az. Of course I want to. I love you, and I don't want you going anywhere. I'm just bummed because summoning you would mean I'd have power over you again, and I don't want that," I said.

To my surprise, Az rolled his eyes. Shaking his head, he met my eyes, his red ones looking unbelievably soft. "Elijah, I haven't felt powerless once. You've given me more freedom than I've ever had, and I want to be bonded to you. I like belonging to you," he said, and then ducked his head, like he hadn't meant to say that last part. I knew how difficult it still was for him to share how he was feeling, so I was glad he hadn't kept that to himself.

"Just as long as you know that I belong to you too," I murmured, and he smiled softly.

"How did you figure it out anyway? And didn't you once say a person could only summon a particular demon once?" I asked, and the look on Az's face now read embarrassed, which was weird. Why was he embarrassed?

"Uh, apparently, that's not true. Fressia dropped by today, and she told me I'd been lied to, though I think the demon who told me that believed it himself, so I don't think he meant to. Anyway, you can summon me again," he explained, and I hugged him again, burying my face into the crook of his neck and pressing soft kisses to the skin there.

"I'm so so happy to hear that," I mumbled against his skin as his arms tightened around me even more.

After a few minutes, he touched the side of my face, and I pulled back to look up at him. He kissed me again, and I lost myself in his touch, in the way his tongue flicked against my lips, urging me to open up for him. We made out for lord knew how long, and then Az pulled back, his pupils wide and his lips red, his face a picture of desire.

"I want you inside me," he whispered, and heat blazed inside me. I reached for him without thought, and he crushed me to him as he attacked my mouth again.

Az stood up straight with me clinging to him, and my feet hovered in the air, my backpack thumping to the floor as he magicked it off me, and he continued kissing me as he led us to the bedroom.

We undressed quickly, swapping kisses between discarding pieces of clothing, and then Az fell onto the bed on his back, pulling me on top.

"I'm ready," he murmured against my lips, and I realized he'd magic-prepped himself, which shouldn't have been this hot but somehow was.

I slid into him in one long thrust, and he moaned loudly, his red eyes shining even brighter. Because of our height difference, I couldn't quite reach his lips in this position, so instead I placed kisses on his sternum, tasting his skin as I slid almost all the way out of him before sinking back in, setting up a maddening pace.

Az flipped us over after a few minutes, and I groaned as he started riding me, his big, muscular body swaying enticingly above mine. I ran my palms up and down his sides as he moved, my eyes trailing over him, admiring all the big and little things I loved about him.

We didn't do this often, but when we did, it was explosive as fuck, and I knew this time would be the same—or maybe even better—as I felt my orgasm closing in, the familiar tingling starting at the base of my spine.

Reaching forward, I wrapped my palm around Az's cock, and he gasped as he quickened his pace, his hole tightening around me. Unable to take it any longer, I pulled him forward. He came willingly, and I pressed my lips to his, sliding my tongue into his mouth. The position was surely awkward for him, but he was too close to care about it.

I came first, filling Az with my cum as I shouted his name, and he followed after me a few thrusts later, painting my chest and abdomen with his release.

Az fell on top of me, and I wrapped my arms and legs around him, hoping to keep him right there for as long as I could. Forever might be a good place to start.

25 | AZAZEL

I USED MY MAGIC to clean us up, not wanting to leave the comfort of Elijah's arms—not that I'd ever admit that to him—and then flipped us over so I wouldn't crush him.

Sex had always been a weird thing for me. As a demon, I'd been around it constantly in the early days, and I'd always been just mildly discomforted by it. I hadn't had a lot of interest in it, and even that tiny smidgen of interest had disappeared after the first time a summoner had used me as her personal sex slave.

Even now, I didn't always feel like it, even when I was physically aroused, even when I had a man whom I loved more than anything in all the realms. I didn't understand why that was, but Elijah did. He said that was just the way I was built, and that as long as I was happy, that was all he cared about. At first, I'd been skeptical, and with good reason. I hadn't seen a lot of human men in their twenties who didn't want sex all the time, but Elijah wasn't a usual human, and I knew that now.

"I know you're a demon and all, but when you make me feel like that, I can't help thinking you're god. Or at least an angel,"

Elijah said, crossing his arms over my chest and resting his chin on them so he could watch me.

I rolled my eyes at him, secretly pleased I'd made him feel that good. "There's no such thing as angels," I said, and he raised a brow.

"So there is a god?" he asked disbelievingly, and I shrugged. That was a minefield I stayed far away from. Humans were weird when it came to religion—not to say they weren't generally a weird bunch.

Elijah chuckled, and I smiled, my eyes roaming over his face. I'd spent the last few weeks desperately cataloging each and every thing about him, afraid I'd lose him and never get to be with him again. At least not until he passed. Then, I could've followed him into Afterworld, but I still would've had to wait decades, and he could've found someone else by then. Someone he loved more than he'd loved me.

"What are you thinking about? Your face is all frowny," Elijah said, and I placed my palm on his back, running it up and down as I tried to figure out what to say.

"Are you sure you want to summon me again? Are you sure you wouldn't rather find a human man? Someone who can grow old with you? I mean, I guess having a demon with magical powers has its perks, but..." I trailed off at the narrow-eyed look on Elijah's face, losing steam.

"You listen to me, and listen carefully," Elijah said, sitting up until he was straddling my stomach. "I love you. I love you more than I've ever loved anyone or anything. I wouldn't care if you lost all your magic tomorrow—I'd still want you. I don't want a human. I don't want your magic. All I want is you. I want the man who gets competitive over arcade games. I want the man who cuddles and watches bad TV with me."

I stared up at him, stunned by the passion in his words. I'd known he loved me—he'd told me enough times to get it through my thick skull—but I hadn't realized how deeply.

"Az, you have no idea what my life was like before you. I was a loner. I had no friends, and pretty much everyone thought I'd turn around and murder someone one day because of my dad. I...I was just existing, Az. I'd forgotten how to live. And then you came, and I promised to show you the wonders of the human world, and somehow, you ended up reminding me what it was to live. You saved me, Az, but more than that—you loved me. I've never been loved the way you love me, and I would never, ever want to give up what we have."

I nodded slowly as something wet touched my ear. Frowning, I touched the spot and realized my cheek was wet. My eyes widened as I realized there were tears on my face, and I quickly scrubbed them away, as if Eli hadn't already seen them.

I squeezed my eyes shut in embarrassment and sucked in a sharp breath when I felt lips brush against the wetness on my cheeks. "It's okay," Elijah murmured, so close I could feel his breath washing over me. "It's okay to cry, Az. It's okay to *feel*."

My eyes opened of their own accord, and I blinked, more tears flowing out. Meeting Elijah's eyes, I realized he had tears in his too, and I reached up to wipe them away, my voice lost somewhere in the maelstrom of emotions inside me.

Elijah leaned closer, and then his lips brushed against mine, so soft, so warm. I pulled him to me, pressing our chests together as I kissed him, my fingers sliding into his silky curls. I still wasn't quite sure why I was crying, but I trusted Elijah enough to not hide from him, to let myself *feel* all these emotions, emotions that I hadn't believed demons were able to feel at all. Maybe Elijah had changed me somehow, on a cellular—or rather magical—level.

A little while later, Elijah pulled back, a small smile on his lips. He kissed my cheek before sliding onto the bed. I turned on my side to face him better and wrapped an arm around his waist, not willing to let him go any further.

"I'm so glad I won't lose this," Elijah murmured, a heaviness in his voice that I recognized as exhaustion. He'd looked tired when he'd walked into the apartment, and everything since must've only added to his tiredness.

"Me too. How about you take a nap and we'll celebrate with a nice dinner later?" I asked, and he smiled softly as he pressed his face into my chest.

"Good idea. Love you," he mumbled, already half asleep.

"Sweet dreams, love," I whispered, pressing a kiss into his curls and settling in for however long he slept. "I'm glad I won't lose this either."

EPILOGUE

Elijah

Trying to summon a demon in the middle of my bedroom probably wasn't a good idea.

Especially when I'd already done it once before. Weren't we supposed to learn from our past? But then again, when had I ever?

At least I'd foregone the salt circle this time. See?

I had set the mood better this time, though. I'd placed nice candles on the coffee table in the living room that smelled like lavender, and I had a bunch of shows lined up on the TV. One was even about a demon.

I placed the journal on the floor and settled in front of the spot I'd cleared, mumbling the spell to myself to get into the groove of speaking Latin. It'd been a year since I'd used the spell, and I didn't want to make any mistakes. There was also a tiny part of me worried last time had been a fluke and I wouldn't be able to do it again, but I pushed that voice to the back of my head and focused on the spell.

I took a deep breath, cleared my throat, and started the spell. After the first stanza, I paused, holding my breath, but nothing happened. I distinctly remembered the way the air had thickened when I'd done the spell last time. Was I my fear going to be proven true?

The words to the second stanza still stumbled out of my lips, and I kept going, even though the room stayed the same around me, even though there was no hellish heat in the air.

The spell ended, and I gasped loudly, my eyes trained on the floor before me. I bit my lip as nothing happened, as the floor didn't shake beneath me, as smoke didn't billow out of a hole in my fucking bedroom.

I'd failed, hadn't I? Azazel wasn't coming back.

I buried my face in my hands, trying my best to keep the tears at bay. I'd try again, and again until I did it, until I got Az back.

"Hey, little human," an achingly familiar voice said, and my head snapped up, eyes widening when I saw him. He was dressed in the same clothes he'd been wearing yesterday, when he'd slowly disappeared before my eyes. He'd told me to wait a day just so there weren't any complications, and I had.

"Az?" I asked, and he raised a teasing brow.

"Were you hoping for a different demon?"

I leaped to my feet and ran over to him, throwing my arms around him. He hugged me back just as tightly, but then pulled back, his lips tugging up on one side.

"You need to offer me a deal, Eli. There's a bit of a time crunch on this thing, you know," he said, and I blinked, remembering we were in the middle of the spell.

"Oh, right," I said, stepping back. Then, I took his hands in mine and looked up into his beautiful red eyes.

"Azazel, here's the deal: how about you become mine for the rest of my life, and in return I promise to love you with my whole heart and spend every day of that time showing it to you?"

Azazel

The rest of his life? I'd expected Elijah to offer a deal for a few years, a decade maybe. I stared at him, eyes wide and mouth open, and his smile flickered.

"Az? Do you want to negotiate?" he asked softly, and I shook my head. I was surprised, not an idiot.

"I accept your deal, little human," I murmured softly, and the widest, happiest smile spread on his lips. He went to throw his arms around me, but then paused.

"Is it done, or is there something left?" he asked, and I smirked.

"A kiss to seal the deal?" I suggested, and he grinned before leaping at me. I kissed him the moment he was close enough, my eyes fluttering shut the moment our lips touched. The time I spent away from him had been the longest twenty-four hours of my life.

I'd spent the whole time visiting all the demons currently living in the human realm since they were the only ones who could see me when I was incorporeal, and even when I'd been talking to them, all my thoughts had been filled with Elijah.

"I missed you," I murmured against his lips, and he smiled, looking up to meet my eyes.

"I missed you too," he said, then tilted his head. "Why didn't the floor open when you showed up this time? I thought for a moment I'd fucked something up and you weren't coming."

I squeezed him tighter in response to the fear in his voice and said, "Two reasons. First, I was in the human realm already, so it took less magic to appear here. Second—and this is the main one—I only did that to scare whatever pesky supe was summoning me because I knew I'd end up accepting their deal, and I wanted them to be at least a little bit scared of me so they wouldn't force me to do shit I didn't want to. It doesn't always work, but sometimes it does. It didn't work with you last time," I said, and he frowned.

"What are you talking about? I was scared as shit," he said, and I chuckled.

"And yet your first order to me was to get a shower," I reminded him, making him laugh. "What's it going to be this time?"

Elijah watched me for a moment, a soft smile on his face. "Stay. For as long as you want me," he said, and I smiled, placing a reverent kiss on his forehead.

"Forever, then," I said with a tilt of my head, and he smiled again.

"Now, how about you and me cuddle on the couch and watch the next season of *MasterChef*?" he asked, and I grinned. Our version of *MasterChef* watching involved me magicking up any dish we thought looked delicious and then judging it for ourselves.

"That sounds perfect," I agreed, and then I followed my little human into the living room for an evening of cuddles and good food as our new bond settled between us, eager to start our forever.

JOIN ME ON PATREON!

Join me on Patreon and get exclusive access to:

- Access to my **first drafts**. (three new chapters every week!)

- Read an exclusive serial, ***The Prince's Mate***.

- Access to audiobooks before everyone else. Listen to **all my audiobooks** for just $12!

- Ability to **make important decisions** about my upcoming books

- Special bonus scenes and **peeks into the lives of old characters**

- Early blurb and cover reveal

- Ability to **create your own character** that I'll write into a book

- **Exclusive merch**: stickers, prints, mugs, and more!

<u>Join Stella on Patreon at patreon.com/authorstellarainbow</u>

ALSO BY STELLA

PARANORMAL ROMANCE

Set in Mistvale

Mages of Ravenshire:
Set in the fictional town of Mistvale, Mages of Ravenshire is a series filled with magic, laughs and love. Low on angst and high on sweetness, Mages of Ravenshire will leave you with a smile on your face. Come meet Neya, Pads, April, and all the other fur-babies and their humans, vampires and mages. *If you're new to the town of Mistvale, this is where you start!*

Touch of Magic. (Raphael x Jai)

Sleep of Eternity. (Cassian x Gus)

Angel of Death. (Aeron x Niall)

Boxset.

Misfits of Mistvale:
With side-characters from Mages of Ravenshire, this series features shifters, half-mermen, werewolves, and many more supernaturals. With the usual dose of fur-babies, found family, and all the Mistvale feels, this series features standalones with a different couple in each book.

Claws. (Devon x Oliver)

Tails. (Jules x Firey)

Bonds. (Joy x Quill x Tate)

Boxset.

Mistvale Spin-Off Novellas:

Featuring various side-characters from the town of Mistvale, these novellas are full of sweet, fluffy romance, and the meddlesome cast of Mistvale.

My Elf Mate. (Noel x Caleb)

My Dragon Mate. (Raiden x William)

My Elf Daddy. (Daddy/little, Westley x Birch)

My Fae Mate. (Genderfluid MC, Celeste x Hector)

Make A Wish. (Free read, Kezan x Ezra)

Christmas In Mistvale. (Revisit ALL your favorite Mistvale couples and see how they're doing!)

The Mistvale Spin-off Collection (Includes My Elf Mate, My Dragon Mate, My Elf Daddy, and My Fae Mate.)

Mystics of Mistvale:
Featuring some new residents of Mistvale, this series includes a single dad incubus, an elusive griffin, a wise unicorn, a protective gargoyle, and some more unique supes. And of course, you'll revisit some of your beloved Mistvalers from the previous books. With the usual dose of romance, found family,

and all the Mistvale feels, this series features standalones with a different couple in each book.

The Elusive Griffin.

The Vulnerable Human.

Set in Otherworld

Fate's Gambit Trilogy:
Fate's Gambit is an MMM PNR trilogy featuring a sweet, subby cinnamon-bun devil, a gentle-giant who's a service sub/Daddy switch, and a slightly frustrated Master as they slowly figure our their dynamic and fall madly in love. They're joined by annoyingly awesome side-characters including a sweet hedgehog, a sassy talking snake, and a guardian in the form of a cat-man. This trilogy features the same triad: **Damien, Reece, & Artemus**, and needs to be read in order.

First Play. (Free Prequel.)

Devil's Gamble.

Pet's Ploy.

Master's Design.

Boxset.

Lords of Otherworld:
Following the events of Fate's Gambit, Lords of Otherworld delves deeper into the workings of Otherworld, with new characters, new romance, and new adventures. With found family vibes, danger and romance, each book in this series follows a different couple, with an overarching storyline. It is recommended to read the books in order.

Maximus

Zane.

Nox.

Lionel.

Set in The Human Realm

Innocent Monsters:
Set in the human realm, this series is a spin-off from the Lords of Otherworld series, featuring the monsters you met in Nox. Find out how the wendigo, kraken, wyvern, troll, and kelpie find their HEA in this series. All books are standalones and can be read in any order.

Salvation.

Liberation.

Conviction.

Standalones

Summoning Chaos (A demon x human novella.)

He Set Me Free (A newsletter serial.)

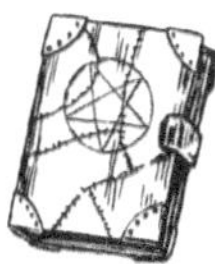

CONTEMPORARY ROMANCE

Voice Out

Weathering The Storm (Roommates to lovers, hurt/comfort.)

Watching The Sunrise (Friends to lovers, genderfluid MC.)

Weaving The Stars (Roommates to lovers, age gap, drag performer MC.)

AUDIOBOOKS

(Available in multiple audiobook stores!)

Lords of Otherworld

Maximus

Zane.

Nox.

Lionel.

ABOUT STELLA

Stella Rainbow lives in a small town in India with her family and her five-year-old cat, Harry, who is her number one supporter, cuddle buddy, and writing buddy all rolled into one. Living with a chronic illness, Stella grew up with books as her best friends, and now she writes in the hopes of giving others like her a reprieve from the real world.

Stella's books are low on the angst, high on the sweetness, with a doze of found family, and some absolutely adorable fur—and sometimes scale—babies.

You can join her <u>mailing list</u> to receive updates about her books and free content. You can also read more about Stella, her books, and the universe she writes in on her website, <u>www.authorstellarainbow.com</u>.

If you'd like to hang out with her, you can also join her Facebook group, **Stella's Mistvalers**.

Subscribe to her **Patreon** to get access to her books as she writes them, get audiobooks at heavily discounted prices, exclusive stories, and much more!

You can also follow her on:
Facebook: <u>Stella Rainbow</u>
Goodreads: <u>Stella Rainbow</u>
BookBub: <u>Stella Rainbow</u>
Amazon: <u>Stella Rainbow</u>